# *Marilyn Pavlovsky*

# BURNING SUNSHINE

# BURNING SUNSHINE
## Author
Marilyn Pavlovsky

- LOOK for these titles that complete the 3 books
about 'The Tragedies of the Dahl's' –

# HONORABLE LIFE
## &
# THE REVERENDS DAUGHTER

**BURNING SUNSHINE**
Copyright © 2008  by  Marilyn Pavlovsky
Standard Copyright License  All rights reserved.
Rights Owner: Marilyn Pavlovsky
Publisher:       Marilyn Pavlovsky
Edited by:       WRGA/Edit - S. Short, Editor
Language:        English
Country:         United States
Edition:         First Edition
Version:         14
Storefront:      ID:4547865 LuLu Publishing
Web-Site         www.book-burningsunshine.com

Library of Congress Catalog Number 2008944363

ISBN 978-0-615-25990-1

## Dedication

I dedicate this book to my wonderful
family
My love and many thanks to my loved
ones who either contributed to, or
supported this effort

*"When they hugged, Rebecca got a mouth full of feathers. Both girls laughed as this brought back so many wonderful memories. "*

# Chapter 1

On a frosty December morning in the year of 19 and 21, a little curly headed boy was born to John and Rebecca Dahl. They named him James, James George to be exact. He was born on a small farm in the foothills of Ohio. Rebecca looked down at her beautiful little son and said,

"You will be my very favorite of all my children."

Of course she remembered saying this very same thing to each and every one of the already six children. Rebecca did not believe the names James and George went together. However, her husband John came from a long line of very respectable and what he considered famous people who were named these names.

Rebecca would get a flippant feeling and want to scream that her family was also very respectable. As for local history she would have never heard much of Ohio, much less ended up there had it not been for the family members of her father's side. She had lived her late teenage years with her Aunt Amy in the foothills of Ohio. Aunt Amy was a farmer's wife. Even so, Miss Rebecca and Aunt Amy could have fit just fine with the elite of Southern Ohio. They could proudly say many of their family members had been a very big part of this small community's history. One member of their family had been the instrumental force behind the design of the water process works. Rebecca had never dwelled much upon these subjects. All she knew was that her family members were all up-standing citizens in their own right. Someone owned the local newspaper. One was a congressman. One close relative was the mayor of the local county seat at one time. One had been a judge and so on and so on. Thank God, some were still alive when Rebecca arrived to the community. She had now been blessed to get acquainted with those left of her Ohio relatives. She must have been too young to care when their careers were being discussed, because she could hardly remember anything she had been told of these individual's life styles. She now would like to hear the history of her Ohio family. Now there was so very few of them left to tell her anything.

Rebecca looked at her handsome new son and said,

"You will do great things young man. I just know you will because you came from such good stock."

She then proceeded to count his little curled up toes, while saying the little rhyme,

"This little piggy went to market and this little piggy stayed home."

She was laughing and loving on this beautiful little baby boy named James George.

Rebecca knew much about the New Orleans side of her family. They too were pillars of their community. Her mother was born and raised in New Orleans, Louisiana. One of the only reasons

8

she knew anything about her father's loved ones was because while searching in an old trunk for a purse of her mothers, she found obituaries. This was long after she was grown. The obituaries were about her grandfather and the others. Many family members were in the Civil War. Some were Colonels and others were Captains. Each obituary started out by saying,

"An Old Solider Died."

Those still alive and still in high positions were just now getting to know Rebecca. Her immediate family never spoke much about these people because they had lived so far away. She would see some of her father's side of the family on holiday, but those visits were rare and far between. She knew this had to distress her loving father.

Rebecca's family had not put much stock into the solider part of one's title. Other than calling someone Colonel so and so, there was not much discussion about such things. She believed this was mainly because her family was split between the north and the south during the Civil War. She also had some relatives in the Revolutionary War, just the same as John.

As wars go, Rebecca was very sure the Civil War had caused her family much pain. She can remember on some family visits of how many relatives had conditions that were caused by injuries of warfare. She also remembered pictures of family members in uniform and remembered how the elders kept telling the children not to dwell on the Civil War. Questions a child would ask would just be answered by an elder saying,

"Because it was a terrible, terrible thing."

9

Then many times they would just shake their heads in sorrow. Another answer a child would get to his questions was,

"That war was where brothers killed brothers."

Rebecca knew two of her great uncles had fought on opposite sides and both had died during that war. She had heard this story many, many times. So, she knew as a child that these stories would make everyone very sad. She now wished she had retained enough of that information to know the complete history of her family to pass on to her children. Even in school she was not very fond of history. So, why did she expect herself to know so much about her own family history?

The baby was already named James George. So, why even think about it? She needed to let this go! In John's eyes one's family history was of so much importance. Rebecca felt a little let down when hurtful thoughts crossed her mind,

"If naming for family greats, why had they not named one of their boy's first name Henderson?"

Her father's name was Henderson. After much discussion she and John had plugged it in the middle of their third son's name. She had forgiven John for this, but she had not forgotten it. In all fairness John had not ask her to name a child after his father either. This was most probably because he had a brother named Andrew and he was named after his father. Maybe that would have been too painful for John anyway because his father had died. He had been dead for several years now. His grandfather had the same name of Andrew and he had died in that terrible Civil War.

The children had been told that this grandfather was buried somewhere in Tennessee.

There sure were enough names to pick from in both families. Rebecca's grandparents and relatives names could have been used too. Who better to name one after than a Captain of the Civil War or some of the Colonels?

Rebecca knew that John's family had migrated from the great State of Virginia. Some of her ancestors were born in Virginia as well and later moved to Southern Ohio. John's family names were just everywhere. A Captain in his family married the daughter of still another Colonel, causing one of the dirt roads that met in front of the house to be called that Colonel's last name. Obviously these families were surely all so mixed up by now.

Rebecca started thinking on the lighter side, while laughing at herself over how the families probably were all relatives now anyway. Why on earth would one want to name a child after anybody anyhow? Each child is their own little person. These thoughts made Rebecca giggle and lessened the bitterness she was feeling towards John over the name. John would not agree with her cute little idea of how she would have liked to have named all of the boys with a name that started with a D. She told him they all could have been D. D.'s. Oh well, she was just as sure someone other than John in that great Dahl family would also disagree with that cute idea. John's family was not very modern in any sense of the word.

As Rebecca rocked her newest addition to the family, she tried to remember everything she must someday tell her son. Things like how the

11

Dahl family had started in Ohio when a Colonel of the Revolutionary War had been amongst the Virginians who fought in a battle with the Shawnee Chief Cornstalk. That battle had taken place in Point Pleasant, West Virginia. One of the Colonel's brothers and two of his sisters had been kidnapped by the Shawnee Indians and they were taken up a long way into Ohio by way of the Raccoon Creek. His Brother was later released. Rebecca had earlier believed the sisters were killed or had to stay on with the Indians. She just wasn't sure. She would have to ask John again. She later believed they too were released and maybe Indians had killed some other sisters while still in Virginia, or something like that. Rebecca never did get that bit of John's history correct. She knew there was something about two girls being killed on the Lewis plantation, thus causing them to be relatives to the Lewis family. Somebody named English Bill had married a Lewis. This man was John's great or great-great grandfather.

Rebecca was sure great things had happened to other families during those early times. Everything done in the United States must have been done by that little hand full of people from a small area in Virginia. Anyone ever mentioned from there had done something extra special to make American's history. Both of their families had been involved with all the happenings and the developing of the good old U.S.A. She must surely study up on all of that. Now as an adult she could see the importance of passing all of this information on to her children. She was sure this would make them very proud of their heritage.

"Strange time in life to become interested in history!"

12

Rebecca thought as she laughed at herself. Thankfully she now knew most of the explanation of how the Dahl family arrived in Southern Ohio. She should! It was discussed at every luncheon or dinner party held at the Dahl's. Sometimes she wondered why everyone did not just live for now! Here and now! They seemed so involved with their history to where she felt they almost had no lives themselves. Of course she knew she was just being cruel because that was not true at all. They had a big wonderful, happy family. She did really love to go over to their homes and cherished all the good times they had together.

The baby was asleep now so Rebecca tried, as if studying, to remember everything. John had told Rebecca of how his great uncle, the brother of the Colonel Grandfather was later called Indian something. John was later to learn this brother was also a grandfather. But that was a more silent history and needed explained more thoroughly, or so she thought. Cousins twice removed somehow married or something. Oh well, who knows? She believed the name of this person to be 'Indian John'. He was given this nickname because of his capture by the Indians. This information she needed to retain because that is where John received his name. Indian John was the first white man to ever see this part of the country. He went back to Virginia and told of how beautiful the countryside was in the Southern Ohio Valley. So somewhere after 1783 when the nation was unable to pay his grandfather or grandfathers for the services rendered to their country, the U.S. offered them land. They chose land in Southern Ohio.

John's still greater grandfather; 'English Bill Dahl' was an Englishman who never got back
13

to Jolly Old England. He had settled in Virginia. Therefore the Dahl's also being from Virginia gave their son Mr. George Dahl a chance to meet and marry the Colonel's daughter. This couple was already married upon the family's arrival to Southern Ohio. The couple came along by wagon train. The whole family had packed up baggage, their children, animals and their lives and moved to Southern Ohio. Rebecca could relate to this because it was just as she and her immediate family had done more recently.

Rebecca's father being an original Ohioan had met her mother who was from Louisiana. Her parents had met while her mother and her family were on a holiday trip. The vacation package had included stopping at all the small cities along the Ohio River. The boat would stop and the passengers would spend a day, sometimes two days or at least the better part of a day at each stop. The parents had met in Gallipolis, Ohio and fell in love. Rebecca's father then followed her mother home at a later date and married her. In later years Rebecca's family traveled this route many times. Having relatives in the Ohio Valley, they would end their trip in the small town and catch the boat on its return back down the river. Although her mother's father had loved and respected her father, there were always the jokes like,

"Look what followed us home!"
He would then spit out a phrase,
"A Yankee!"

Rebecca now having seven children of her own by Mr. Dahl was living on about forty-six acres of some of the original Colonel's land. Of course she had already met many of the older Dahl family members. Her in-laws were just one farm away. She lived at forks in the road and 'Gee Whiz', one of these roads was named after John's brother. A whole little village just two miles the other way down the road was named after the Colonel. All they did when naming that little village was to add a –(ton) to the end of the family name.

Rebecca did not mean to be sinister with any of her little bitter thoughts. She did seriously love this big loving family, but she had heard these famous stories over and over and over again. This family was so-o-o-o proud of their heritage. Thus, causing this beautiful little baby boy lying in front of her to forever be branded with a name like James George Dahl. Rebecca tried to think happy thoughts by saying to herself,

"OH FORGET THE NAME, as handsome as this little man is he will never have a problem with anyone. Besides, look at those large beautiful hands. He is going to be so muscular and so strong; no one will ever dare mess with him."

Every finger, every toe, his little nose, his deep-deep blue eyes were all so perfect upon this wonderful little bundle of joy. He had such beautiful blonde curls that you could pull one out to the end and it would just spring back into place. Had he not been so strong with muscles he would have surely been mistaken for a girl, but not once had anyone done that. Babies little tiny features always griped the very strings of Rebecca's heart. She needed to quit putting so much stock into his messed up name.

# Chapter 2

Life up to this point had not been very easy for Rebecca. She had lost so much and yet you could say she had gained a lot too. She now had such a loving husband and such beautiful healthy children. Just last year she and John had been able to buy the one-hundred and eighty acres adjoining their little farm. It did help that it belonged to another family member at the time of the purchase. Rebecca believed they really got a good deal. This increased their farming space to over two-hundred acres. They were blessed. Yes, truly blessed!

Yet, Rebecca's memories would often wonder back to her childhood by the city of New Orleans where she lived with her mother, father, sisters and a brother. The land down there was so vivid in her memories. One never knew where the borders of her parent's land were. All she knew was the land was massive. She and her family members enjoyed parties in their lovely home. She became aware later that the northern people called these homes 'southern mansions'. John would often tease her about her spoiled life style. Her childhood was so far removed from the lifestyle she now lived in this hard working Ohio land.

Although Rebecca was very modest, many people had told her parents that their daughters were very beautiful. Rebecca really believed the others were probably beautiful and they were. Her sister Beatrice would always say,

"Rebecca, you are the pretty one."
Rebecca would then say,

"No you are the pretty one."
The girls and their dashing family were forever being invited to wonderful dinner parties in the pretty city of New Orleans. Things she had taken for granted as a child, she now realized was not so normal in the rest of the world. Everyone does not live as her family had lived. The homes of their friends and extended family members were probably also considered by others to be mansions. The pillars and long steps were so common-place in her home town. They were also very common in all of the New Orleans surrounding areas.

Rebecca's home had six pillars reaching high into the third floor roofing. Each room had a fireplace, many tapestries and beautiful wood carvings. A large winding wide stairway made its way from the front door to the second floor where there was a landing that connected to four bedrooms. Then the stairway twisted and turned again and went on to the third floor. On the third floor there were still another four bedrooms. It is a wonder someone was not killed while sliding down those banisters. To Rebecca and the other children, sliding down the banisters was a favorite form of entertainment. Each of the girl's rooms was stuffed with pretty clothing made of fine silks and linens. Rebecca of course, loved her old home place and missed it very much.

A house is only a house until a family makes it a home, no matter what size it is. Rebecca knows that now. She and her husband had made this modest little farm house into a home. She thanked God her mother and her father had also made that large mansion a home. She let her mind wonder as she thought of her richer life. If she missed any of that rich life, she probably missed her beautiful clothing most. She really missed the magnolia trees with their big white blooms and fragrant smells. She missed the moss growing on the other trees, giving them a majestic site just as evening approached, or as the sun shined through that moss during the day. She missed all of the smells and all of the beauty remembered from her childhood. In all honesty in her deepest of thoughts, members of her family and the servants who truly in her heart were just some extension of her family troubled her the most. She often had a hard time dealing with their loss. The biggest material miss was most probably the beautiful gowns, shoes and other fineries afforded her due to the status of their wealth.

Rebecca snapped back into reality as she looked down at her beautiful new born son and thought to herself.

"Why is your mother remembering such things? I am so rich! I'm rich beyond anyone's riches. I have you, your father, your sisters and brothers. What wonderful miracles! What more could one wish for."

Yet knowing she would forever miss her family and the days gone by. Rebecca wished her husband and children could have known all the
19

people of her family, those still alive and those who are now deceased. After all these years it seemed as if that life was someone else's life. Those loved ones still living were now so far away. She felt she would never see them again.

On a nearby dresser was a tin picture in a small glass frame. In the picture were Rebecca's sisters, Eva, Bea and herself. Tears started to form in the corner of her eyes as she looked at that picture. She did miss her family so very much. The longer she looked at the tiny picture she started to smile as her thoughts wondered backwards,

"I wonder if I could still fit into that dress. That dress was so beautiful."
It was a beautiful full velvet wine colored gown that had stiff slips to go under it. It had a very tiny waste line. She noticed she was talking to herself by saying,

"Probably not silly, you had six children and now you just gave birth to another. And, this baby is a very large little man."
She then broke into laughter as she looked at the picture more closely. Those tall feathers attached to Eva's hat needed to go. She remembers how she and Bea joked that day of the setting. They teased about the feathers and of how they would take up the whole tin. Stating there would not be any room left on the tin for their faces. Needless to say by the time they got to the setting, Eva was definitely ready to get it all over with. They had teased her the whole way of the carriage ride. Eva being two years younger than Rebecca, the older girls loved to tease her. She remembered the day of the setting so well. Wait a minute she thought,

"I loaned those earrings and necklace to Eva. *That Brat!*"
Those earrings were hand cut from liberty dimes. Holes were cut inside the rings outlining around the liberty statue. Where could they be? Rebecca had begged her father for this ensemble even when he was not in the mood to purchase trinkets for her. She would always remember watching his face the minute she knew she had melted his heart.

"Okay Beck,"
as he often called her,

"I can see where this would be lovely on your pretty little head and that neck."
He then took her neck into his big hands, joking like he was going to choke her. Where is that beautiful set? She must write Eva and ask. She would bet the little stinker had never returned them. She had an afterthought of how sisters are wonderful until you cannot find your belongings!

Speaking of sisters, where was Mary in that picture? Maybe she was just too small for this outing or just did not want to accompany her sisters to a picture take. She must have stayed with Mabel. She, out of all the siblings had stayed within hem distance of her nanny ever since her birth. When leaving for Ohio; leaving Mabel behind was one of the hardest things to do. It had to be done because she had her own biological family, but this was not an easy task. Those facts did not make it any easier to leave her. This had to be one of the hardest things to do for each child. Oh she wrote all the time, but being fairly uneducated and getting older, you could hardly make out anything she had to say in her letters except the part of how much she loved each and every one. That was always very clear. Mabel was missed terribly by everyone.

James let out a little whimper bringing his mother back into this day and time. Being a poor farmer's wife; transportation at best would be a horse and a buggy. John had managed to purchase a side saddle and a very pretty little white carriage. It had white fringe hanging all around the top of it. He had purchased these items for Rebecca as wedding gifts while they were still in Columbus, Ohio. The carriage was probably way too different of an item for the farm community that surrounded them, but it was something Rebecca loved. She loved it if for no other reason than because her husband had given it to her. Could she go visiting by herself? Probably not, in these parts of the country there was no such thing as a carriage driver. You either took the reins yourself or you stayed home. How many years she thought, had it been by now that she had not seen her sisters and her brother Dale?

James dozed off into baby sleepy land and Rebecca thought of the chores to do. Since having James, everyone was so protective of her. Someone had most surely finished all the chores by now anyway. Everyone wanted to give her some rest. She stretched out onto the bed beside her sleeping son and just let her mind wonder back to a spring day from her youth. Although it was now winter in Ohio, she had opened the window ever so slightly to let in a little fresh air. As her pretty lace curtains blew inward from a mild breeze, she was remembering that lovely spring day that she, her brother and her sisters arrived on the banks of the Ohio River. She remembered getting off their beautiful, comfortable river boat to land in a small French City called Gallipolis. The steam organ or calliope was playing. The people around them were laughing and everyone seemed oh so very happy. Little did this family know that this would be the last time in their lives they would be treated like royalty! Never again would they enjoy all the comforts afforded. When getting off the riverboat, Rebecca had thought to herself, at least this little city was French so maybe the contrast would not be so drastic.

The trip happened shortly after their father's passing and all the sad happenings that had preceded his death. Was she really only seventeen when all of this happened? She remembered so very well the day they were leaving home and when she and her siblings were getting onto the river boat. They waved goodbye to their uncles and aunts, cousins, the reverend and their servants. One of those waving back at them was their beloved servant, Mabel. She had tears flowing down her face. Mabel had always taken such good care of them. Wiping away many of their tears and doctoring cuts and scrapes were only a few of the many wonderful things Mabel had done for them. She was still wiping away their tears while shedding so many of her own when they lost their mother, then their father.

It seemed as though Rebecca had been a very happy young lady one day. Then she woke up the next day to find herself in a position to where she now must grow up completely. She must take on way more responsibilities and more hurt than any young person should ever have to bear. At least she was older than some of her siblings. Think of the pain and stress it must have caused Mary and Dale. Her mother had died two years prior with what the doctor stated,

"An unknown virus."

Now her father was gone too, but is there any wonder? He had the grief of losing mother. He then had the combination of the largest oil well on the plantation going up in flames, which also caused the death of his right hand man, Jo-Bob. Then top all of that off with the driest season ever recorded that killed every produce or plant they owned. This all happened very shortly after mother's death. How could her father cope with it all? She guesses he didn't do very well coping because he too was now gone.

Rebecca remembers after her mother's death of how her father sat at the half open pit full of ice. He would sit with his feet dangling over the walls. She supposed to stay cool. He would often have his head in his hands. She knew he was crying, but no one would ever dare let him know that they knew this. With Daddy gone now too, the only thing she and Beatrice could do was to sell the house and the land. They then would buy passage on a river boat to go to a family member's home.

Father had an elderly mother in Southern Ohio and he also had a sister in Racine, Ohio. Shortly after their mother's death and all of the bad happenings, the aunt had written a letter to their father. She had stated she would take the younger children for a while to relieve him of so much stress during his rebuild. He refused, stating he needed his children by his side. Bea had since written their Aunt Amy to tell her of their father's death. Rebecca remembered only meeting her aunt once when she was a small child, but it sounded as though she was a very caring woman who would be there in this time of need. She had returned a letter telling Beatrice to please sell everything as her father had requested and to bring the entire family to live with her and her husband.

Rebecca's sister Beatrice whom she called Bea, had already finished high school a couple of years before, but had to delay any further education. Rebecca would have finished high school the year of her father's death. She too had to drop out for a while to help around the house. Each child knew they were expected to continue their education. Therefore Bea would only be staying through the one year at Aunt Amy's farm in Racine, Ohio. She would then find a college to continue her education. The monies collected from the sale of the plantation would have to stretch all the way through five children's education.

The riverboat trip had not been a cheap one either. The girls had packed many things they now knew they would never have any use for in this part of the country. Reflecting back, the girls realized they would have saved some money if they had known this in advance. Rebecca had chosen to bring along mothers organ. She had purchased it for her mother by selling a calf when she was just a young teen and could not see leaving it behind, but things like that just made the boat trip more expensive. The family knew they must now keep close reins on what money they had left.

The first spring in Ohio would be so very different from Rebecca's childhood. It did not take much to figure that out. Their aunt and uncle picked them up at the boat in an old buckboard wagon that needed paint badly. It was pulled by two old worn down horses. Rebecca's family was coming from the pleasures of having servants and pleasantries to an Ohio dirt farm.

The young family had never met Aunt Amy's husband. His name was Richard. He was neither pleasant nor harsh. He just did not have much of anything to say. He had a very full mustache, to where you could not tell if he was smiling or even if he had teeth. But he stood there in an old worn out pair of bibbed overalls that had a patch here and there. Rebecca did however remember thinking the overalls were very, very clean. The petite little aunt had on a very plain cotton dress they would learn later she had sewn for herself. The dress was made from sacks she and Uncle Richard had bought things in, like flour or feed of some sort. The aunt was a pretty, but worn little lady with a smile that would light up the world. She gave very tight happy hugs and they knew they were more than welcome right from the start. Without the love and the warmth of their aunt, the arrival at this dirt farm would have been unbearable. The farm was carved out of the hills and the rocks. Without the love shown there would have been an even bigger shock to this high class family's systems.

The sibling family came to the realization very quickly that their summer would be filled with still more digging for their food and survival. There was no turning back now. How could they? This was their destiny. Aunt Amy was a sweet little lady who was trying so hard to make sure each child knew that she truly cared. She wanted them to know she loved them and that she would always be there for them. She and her husband

26

had no children and Rebecca believed she was a little over-whelmed with the group that she just inherited. She kept apologizing for not having the fineries her nieces and nephew were all so used to. You could tell though, she really was still happy that they were there. Their Aunt Amy would also often break down due to the loss of her beloved brother. One could tell she was going to do everything in her power to make the move for his children as pleasant as she could.

One day in the heat of the afternoon, the girls were hoeing in the garden. Bea and Rebecca were having a long talk to help pass the time and distract themselves from the pains their new lives had brought. They were wondering what life would have been like had they not followed their father's instructions. What would have happened if they had not given their father such a promise while he was on his death bed? If only they could have managed the plantation until Dale became old enough. The girls had promised to sell what was left of the plantation after they gave each servant their cabin and the plot of land that they had been share cropping. They were to give each family a deed to their property and an equal amount of cash to keep them going. This too was done as their father had wished. The family was then to go to their Aunt Amy's where they would help out on the farm and work for their keep. Each child would go off to school one by one, gathering a higher education.

If Dale had been older, their father would have expected him to keep the plantation going. But since the girls were the oldest, he felt he had no choice but to give the instructions he gave. They realized a promise was a promise and they

27

must keep every word of it, no matter how hard or miserable this back breaking work would become.

Father's plan had not been a bad plan until one was exhausted from milking cows at five in the morning, planting vegetables until noon and then plowing the fields until you could not see in the evenings. Taking off your shoes because of blisters after a hard days' work only to step into what the chickens had left behind. To get a drink of water the girls would have to work the large iron pump at the well. A person had to have enough strength left to pump the pump until that person received enough water that would drop into a tin-cup for the person to drink. At home the water was hauled in by servants and remained chilled in large ceramic containers. All one had to do was raise a little handle to get a glass of water when thirsty. It seemed on this farm one would surely die if they did not keep up enough strength to work that pump.

A sad thought crossed Rebecca's mind,
"Those poor servants."
She had never thought of it in that way before. The south had just always had servants. Or, before the war they were called slaves and unpaid for their services. At least after the war those who stayed on with the plantations were paid either by money or what was called share cropping. Rebecca, being born in 1883 was so thankful everything had changed before she was born. She did not think she could have been an owner of a person. How does one own someone? What would it feel like to be owned by someone? Oh, how awful! She guessed the servants were most probably still owned when her mother was a child. She did not feel this made any of her ancestor's

28

bad people. She just realized it was an accepted way of life at the time. Her grandfather had passed away without any sons. Since Rebecca's father had shown so much interest in the plantation it was given to her father and mother by the grandfather.

Rebecca's mother often told of how the Civil War had not much of an effect on their way of living. Slaves at their plantation seemed to be happy. Maybe they were just too afraid to move away because they had lived all of their lives on that land. Yet, everyone seemed very happy to be there. That war had hurt the family otherwise though. For instance, Aunt Amy caring much for her brother had before Rebecca's birth chosen to live with her brother's family in Louisiana. After the war their Aunt Amy had married one of those left over blue coats who forgot to go home until he could figure out a way to steal a southern girl. Of course one could have called father and Aunt Amy north-southern mixtures anyway. The blue coat her father so often joked about was now their beloved Uncle Richard who was raised within almost spitting distance from her father.

The slave families who had stayed on at the plantation were born there. They were definitely as important as Rebecca and her family to the plantation. Their beloved Mabel and all living members of her family were born there. Rebecca would shudder at her thoughts as she imagined the painful feelings these people must have had after doing the kind of work she and her siblings were now doing. Can you imagine how they felt as they lay down at night? The sun was most surely hotter in New Orleans than it would ever be in Ohio. Those people had to work that way from the very day they were born.

29

During the time of their stay at Aunt Amy's, Rebecca remembers one day reaching down to get another plant. She thought of how neither she nor Beatrice had ever allowed their beautiful faces to even see sunshine. Now they were probably getting all crinkled and cracked from the burning outdoors. At least Aunt Amy had provided them with wide rimed bonnets that tied beneath their chins. She also provided an apron that was more like a dress in itself. It had two arm holes and wrapped all the way around ones' body while being tied in the back like a little girl's dress. It had huge pockets for everything from a plow head to a sweat rag. Poor little Mary, the aprons about covered her up head and all. The girls had to laugh when they looked at each other.

The sisters had been on their knees planting tomatoes. Bea had a clump of dirt in her hair and Rebecca had wiped a big dirty mark from her forehead to her mouth. Eva's dress and apron were covered in mud. Bea laughed and said,

"We sure would have a hard time convincing some nice young men we are usually half way pretty women. Thank God we live in a nowhere land miles from everyone. There is no worry of us ever being seen."

Rebecca laughed as she said,

"Are you sure they do not have to pipe sunshine into this place? If so, they could have left the heat part out of it,"

Bea remarked,

"Yeah, I thought the plantation was remote, but this feels more like we are in a foreign country!"

At least the girls kept a sense of humor about their plight. During these short nights the humidity was

30

so high due to the adjoining river. They had to leave windows wide open to cool off enough to sleep. The fog was so thick they could have cut it with a knife. They had never seen such a site. The fog was pretty when the sun came up, but really strange to these southern ladies. At least they did not have the kind of mosquito problems one has in Louisiana.

The only dreams that would make Rebecca's life bearable during these times were those of how she could maybe someday move into the nearby city of Gallipolis and work. Maybe an office job, or work in a store. Many modern day women were going to work on jobs now-of-days and some were making very good money, thus becoming very independent. Of course she guessed she would have to finish school first.

During these times as Rebecca would try to cool off enough to sleep she would sort out her dreams on how her new life was going to be. If she worked, she could get an apartment or room and rest, yes rest. Her thoughts were what she would give for just one day of rest. She may even have time to read a book and maybe she could have some kind of a social life. Oh yes, a social life again. Wouldn't that be grand? A short time before father's death, Bea and the house servants had put together a really nice coming out party for her. What good would that do now? If she wasn't stuck on this remote farm she could maybe meet charming people. She could sing, dance and be merry.

At one time Rebecca's Ohio grandfather had owned a grand home in the old French city. After his death, grandmother had sold it due to her health. She had purchased a small home out in the country a few miles from Aunt Amy. Any monies she had after the sale and the purchase of this little home were being saved for her future upkeep. They knew she would need these monies should she remain stubborn as she was and continue to want to go to what was called an old people's home. Their Cousin Chancy was a young man who was caring for her at present, or she was caring for him. It was hard to tell which. Maybe it was a little of both.

Someone had told Rebecca of how everyone who was anyone in the city of Gallipolis hung out at a French Lord's home. The name of his home was the 'Our House'. It was a bit of a hotel, restaurant and a lounge. She was told the Lord of this home had a large ball room with a wonderful orchestra. He often had many wonderful shows or entertainers performing there. This was where the better class of people gathered to dance and to have fun. The past few months had been filled with so much hard work and dirt. Rebecca's hands were sore and rough and her legs were so tight in the muscles. She wondered should her dreams ever come true would she even be able to dance. Gosh, after a summer like that would she even remember how to dance?

They were also told of a fairly new theatre that had been built in 1895. They called it the 'Ariel Theatre'. Here many big named stars on a circuit came to perform. Her thoughts had been if maybe she could get off of this farm once in a while, it may not be such a backwoods world after all. It would be fun to meet some of the stars. However, she was told there was a tunnel from the hotel to the theatre. This was to keep the stars from being troubled by such fans. In that case the likely-hood of meeting a star would be very rare. None-the-less it would be wonderful to watch just one show.

Aunt Amy had also told the family of a nearby school named Rio Grande College. This college had been founded sometime during 1876. Though growing fast, it was still limited in the courses it offered. It was located just north of Gallipolis, Ohio. She had hoped the children could go there. This was of course depending on the courses they wished to take. The way Aunt Amy saw it, going to this college would give them an opportunity to come back to her farm during the summers. Rebecca's thoughts being that of a normal teenager were pretty harsh. She thought, other than visiting their wonderful aunt and uncle, little sisters and brother, <u>WHO</u> on earth would ever want to do that? Sure, Sure, Sure, go to school all season, then come home and work your fingers to the bone in the summer! <u>WOW</u>, that sounds like a plan to me, she thought!

# Chapter 3

Rebecca dozed off for a while, only to be awakened by James crying for his dinner. She got up with the baby and sat down in the rocking-chair. She dropped the top of her dress and began to feed the hungry little man. She noticed she had been alone with the baby for a considerably long time. Could this be true? Where had all of her guards gone? Mrs. Pinkerton, one of her closest neighbors and her mid-wife, surely had to go home to check on her own family. The other children must have gone to help John with the chores. What could have happened to her mother-in-law who kept insisting she must stay in bed for a full nine days? What was that all about anyway? She felt fantastic! She had felt fantastic after every childbirth. If one had to stay in bed and be pampered for nine days, why didn't someone suggest that you could stay in bed the nine days before the child was born? That's when you are really miserable. She knew this practice was quite common after having a baby, but never could figure out the reason for staying in bed so long. James had fallen asleep again, so she reached over and placed this precious little curly headed baby into his crib.

Rebecca let herself fall back into the chair and continued her remembrance of the past. Her shallow teenage dreams had never come true. In the fall of the second year after arriving to Ohio, she did leave for school as planned. Her sister Beatrice had gone on before her. Her sister, as she would often say (wished to make her life worth something). Therefore, she had chosen to be a nurse. The education she needed at that time was not offered at the Rio Grande College; the college located just above Gallipolis that Aunt Amy had wished for them to attend. In that day so many people had tuberculosis, better known as T. B. Beatrice and Rebecca had often wondered if this was not the disease that had taken their beloved mother from them. This disease was highly contagious and no one else at the plantation came down with it, so possibly that was not the case. The doctor had just said an unknown virus, but one still tries to give reason to an untimely death.

Rebecca can remember days and days on end when Mabel, their house servant and nanny, would lay cool wet towels on her mother's forehead. She would hold their mother's hand while praying to God that he would spare this angel. Big tears would flow down her face to where she looked like an angel herself from the shine the tears would leave. Rebecca stopped to ponder and realized how very much she misses her mother and Mabel. Mabel was really like a second mother even though she had a family of her own. She knew Mabel also loved each and every one of them the same. She too would not be around much longer because she was getting up in years.

36

Rebecca believed mother's death was the deciding factor in Bea's choice of careers. The only college that offered expertise in this field at the time was in Columbus, Ohio. Since monies were to be used sparingly and this sounded like a promising career, Rebecca chose the same education. This was probably for many of the same reasons. She also believed she and her sister would save on expenses by living together.

Rebecca can remember the day that came to leave her Aunt Amy's and how she hated leaving her younger sisters and brother behind. She was of course, happy to know they would be so well taken care of by their wonderful Aunt Amy and Uncle Richard. Eva, Mary and Dale had adjusted quite well and seemed to really enjoy their new home. Dale was becoming quite a little man and traced every foot step that Uncle Richard took. The uncle called him his right hand man. You could tell that both; the uncle and aunt really enjoyed especially the younger children. Not being able to have children themselves, this was like a God send to them. Aunt Amy was disappointed about Bea, then Rebecca going off so far away to school but understood the reasoning.

On the day she was to leave for school, Rebecca was taken to the Gallipolis Train Depot by her uncle. Once again, she traveled on that old worn out buckboard. As her bags were being tossed into the back she thought of how those old horses must not have been in as bad of shape as she had believed at the time she had gotten off that riverboat two years earlier. They were still very much alive and they were still pulling that old buckboard wagon. The wagon still needed painted and the horses still looked worn down but they got the job done.  Uncle Richard was a man of few words, but this day he was exceptionally quiet. She knew he was depressed because she was leaving, so she just left it all alone.

Since the arrival to the valley Rebecca had realized how beautiful it really was around there. So, she talked to her uncle even if he did not answer.  She told him of how pretty she thought the countryside was.  The old uncle just listened, still with that grim looking face as he directed the horses along the bumpy roads.  Upon arrival at the station his demure changed drastically.  Uncle Richard was all nervous.  He was asking things like,

"Do you have your tickets?"

He was saying things in a rapid tone of voice like,

"Do not talk to strange men or people you do not know.  Get off that train and look for Bea immediately."

Calming down long enough to state,

"Tell her we send our love".

Then, immediately throwing in his opinion by saying,

"I do not like her being alone in that big ole' city either."

To have been so quiet on the trip, he sure was full of advice now.  She smiled knowingly at him and thought of how all of his advice was well taken of course.  With a big hug and a fast goodbye Rebecca stepped up the three steps onto her train car.

This trip was so different from the trip to Ohio.  She and her family had often taken boat trips on family outings.  Therefore nothing had been new about that riverboat ride except the distance.  The train trip was nice too.  It was just

38

different in an exciting kind of way. Yes, Rebecca found this trip to be exciting in every way. Part of the excitement of course could have had a little to do with the fact she was leaving that dirt farm. She often thought she would never want to dig in the dirt and out in the sunshine again. She believed if she did, her face would become so weathered that it would surely break if she even attempted to smile. Relief, fear, happiness and excitement all wrapped up into one package seemed to be the feeling Rebecca was having on this trip. She was so looking forward to seeing her sister. Very rough ride though, she would surely be beaten up by the time the train pulled into the Columbus Depot.

When she did finally reach the depot, there was a wonderful reunion between the sisters. How wonderful to see Beatrice again. She looked radiant. When they hugged, Rebecca got a mouth full of feathers from Beatrice's hat. Both girls just broke out laughing as they remembered the day many years ago at the picture making. Rebecca reminded Beatrice of how she must have taken a lesson from their younger sister Eva. Beatrice's hat was very colorful and had feathers standing even higher than those on that hat of Eva's they both remembered so well.

Bea was shorter than Rebecca, but thin and beautiful. Both had taken so much of their looks from their mother. Rebecca's hair seemed to be of a finer texture and grew so much faster than Bea's. Bea could hardly keep hers up because of its length. She was forever tucking her blonde curly hair back up under her hat. Really it looked very cute falling down into curls around her face. But Beatrice hated it and often stated of how she wished she could have taken her hair from her
39

mother's side instead of the curls her father owned. Both girls were petite, I guess one would say. However, Rebecca felt like a giant sometimes because of her height. She was about 5'6 & ½ inches tall. No other woman seemed to be as tall as she during that day and time. They each had sparkling blue eyes and pale porcelain like complexions. The girls probably weighed about one-hundred pounds each. At least Bea could weigh no more than that. Rebecca may have weighed up to one-hundred-ten if soaking wet, as the old saying goes.

Rebecca could probably sit on her hair. All she had to do of a morning was twist it up, put in a pin or two and push it back down. Then she was ready for the day. It was the nights and the washings that took so long. Brushing that hair one-hundred strokes each night was a real job. The washing had to be done with rain water only. She would catch the water off the roof at home. Now she felt the homemade lye soap, the only kind of soap her Aunt Amy had, probably had about destroyed her hair. The old house where her uncle and aunt lived had been white washed somewhere along the way, but now was all black or brown and the roof had rust on it. She remembers worrying about that rust upon the arrival at her aunt's home. Now she thinks maybe the rust was good for her hair. It still, at least shined.

After the arrival to Columbus, Ohio it did not take long to get with the swing of things. For the next two long years Rebecca studied nursing. She met very few people due to the fact she could not afford to leave the campus. Her clothing was getting outdated by now and was wearing pretty thin. She knew she could not spend one cent more than allotted to her since she was only the second child to take advantage of the education money. She and Beatrice were in the same boat of course. The sisters knew there were still Eva, Mary and Dale who would need the same chance at the education they were fortunate enough to receive. The girls became each-others entertainment and even closer than before. It really was wonderful spending her college years staying in a room on campus with her big sister. They had so much in common and had so much fun just being together. They loved each other very much.

Columbus was a very large city. It probably seemed larger to the young ladies because it was so unfamiliar to them. They rarely adventured out to see much of it. They held such tight reins on their purse strings. They had many discussions about the next three children and their education. Now they had heard rumors from other Ohio members of their family that they just could not put to rest. Why had they never been told about Chancy?

Chancy had lived with their grandmother all of his life and they had believed him to be their first cousin. Like so many ghosts in one's closets, this ghost seemed not to appear until after mother and father had both passed away? Rumor has it that Chancy was fathered by their father instead of their father's brother as the siblings had assumed. This meant father had been married before marrying mother and no one bothered to tell them. Chancy's mother had died at child birth. Maybe they had heard something of the sort before, but rumors were always dampened around their home. That, accompanied with the living so far from

41

other members of their father's family may have made it easy for none of the siblings to hear the truth. If these rumors were not true, then why out of the eight children of her uncle's family would their uncle single out Chancy and make him live with his grandparents. These rumors brought up many questions in the sister's minds.

Even though the grandparents had been pretty comfortable in their status of life, could Chancy come in and put a claim to any of the education monies allocated for the girls and their siblings? Rebecca felt there was not enough to go around in regards to education now anyway. The college rates seemed to go up every quarter as it was. Did Chancy know the truth?

Rebecca and her siblings had always felt a special closeness to Chancy. He used to come down the river sometimes for a whole summer. Now that she thinks about it, he felt more like a big brother. They all loved him very much and hated to see him leave when he would get back on the riverboat. To her knowledge, Chancy had never attended a higher education program. The money just could not be stretched that far. Men who wanted an education would receive their education first in most families. Rebecca knew this to be true. Very few young women at the turn of the century received a high school education, much less a college degree. Born in March of 1883, Rebecca knew she was very fortunate in this respect. Very fortunate indeed!

# Chapter 4

Months passed, and Rebecca had gotten back into the routine of raising children. Winter, spring and summer had sped by this year. It was hard for her to believe the harvest time was already here. She placed James into a basket. It was draped with a cheese cloth. She had placed the cheese cloth over the basket to keep out the bugs. She headed for the field they called the corn patch. She had felt kind of down lately, probably some sort of after birth depression or something. Maybe it was the deep longing to see her brother and sisters. She felt sadness come all over her.

"Enough of this,"
she thought! I am just feeling sorry for myself and there is no time for that. She looked out over the field to see her entire clan, as she liked to call her children. Each child was breaking off the ears of corn and shucking each ear with a speed of leopards. She thought of how sore their little hands would be tonight. There was nothing like those beautiful children to snap Rebecca out of her depression. How proud she was as she gazed at this healthy little group she and John had created, or as one would say, brought into this world.

Looking further, she saw the wagon and then she saw John. The heat of the day had caused him to remove his shirt. There he stood, throwing big bags of corn from one end of that wagon to the other. The sun was shining upon his bulging muscles. The muscles were very tan and glistening. Oh, what a handsome man he was. He had beautiful blond hair, a mustache and a build most men would pray for. No wonder she had fallen so head over heels in love with him. She believes that must have happened the very first time she saw him. Not to even mention those beautiful eyes of deep sky blue and a face to frame them that neared a strong beauty. Over the years she learned he also had the most beautiful heart and he was such a loving person. John Dahl, after all these years and with all of the children, could still make her legs go weak with just one look into his eyes. How could any woman be luckier? From the next field the children started waving and screaming,

"Hello Mother!"
Then begged,

"Can we stop and play with James?"
Rebecca caught herself smiling when John did not give her a chance to answer. Instead he stated in that deep stern voice,

"Hey, Hey, dark is coming, you will have time to play with James after dinner."
Then those words he was so famous for,

"You don't work, we don't eat!"
He always added,

"A little work never killed anyone."
Each child gave a little groan and a sigh but went right back to work like good little soldiers. Rebecca wondered why the children never really
44

listened to her quite in that way, thinking sometimes she may let them run all over her. She believed she did that because she often felt it was so hard for her children. They had to work so hard. She prayed they at least would grow up knowing they are very much loved.

"Oh my,"
she thought,
"I still have to cross another field and this basket is getting heavier with every step."
James had grown so and her poor old body was not what it used to be. Should she be feeling like this at the ripe old age of thirty-five? She hoped she did not look as badly as she felt. Everyone had always told her how beautiful she was as a girl. She always felt it was only because she was one-half French and was fortunate enough to have a good standing in life. She really felt her sisters were prettier. In reality Rebecca was probably the best looking of all the siblings. All of the sisters were very pretty young ladies, but none stood as statuette and none had the smooth lines that Rebecca received. Her parents had taught modesty very well, because she did not realize that she was a very beautiful woman. She was tall and thin. She had light brown hair that flowed down the middle of her back. It hung way below her tiny waist. Her tiny face and high cheek bones made for a very beautiful woman.

As she neared the field, she knew she would work in this field until it came time for cooking dinner. The dinner would be cooked on that old hot, wood cook-stove and the kitchen would feel as though the whole room was an oven. As usual, she remembered the summer kitchen of her childhood. It was away from the house and
45

usually only the servants would work in it. Why does she think of such things? It only makes her feel guilty and ashamed that she is not more appreciative of what she has. Past is past. Here and now is where she wants to be. She wants to be with her beautiful children and that handsome husband. John had just built onto the house. He built a beautiful kitchen that had doors across from each other. This was done for ventilation. He had included two large windows. This increased the size of the home so much and had made it more comfortable for the ever growing family. Feeling guilty, she looked toward heaven and said,

"Thank you God for my many blessings and forgive me if I complain about the hard work and hardships we have. I am so sorry,"

The Dahl's worked that farm every day of every week except Sundays when they would only do what was necessary to keep their livestock alive. They thanked God for the food He placed upon their table. Their off hours were spent with the larger children bathing themselves then bathing or helping with the bathing of the younger children. During school months the older children would get their lessons and then they would help their mother study with the younger children. Rebecca tended to her children, her mending, her house and her husband. John would read to the children. He would read the Bible and other books while everyone would gather around an oil lamp. They would then get on their knees and join hands in a family circle for an evening prayer.

Sundays they would walk, ride a wagon or a sleigh to a little old log church in the family named town two miles up the road. For the Dahl family a church gathering was not something you would miss unless you were near death's door. The Dahl's were raised so very different from Rebecca's raising. John's family had always been farmers. Although one would probably not consider them really poor due to the owning of so much property. They were still poor. This was the normal for these farm people. John would often joke by saying his family was poor, clean and God fearing.

The Dahl's religion was very different from the quiet New Orleans church Rebecca had known as a child. Her church had been a gathering place for the elite of New Orleans. It had beautiful stained glass windows, shining brass and bright wood floors. Often her church felt more like a fashion show than a church meeting. This was because the ladies would show off their New York hats and the latest styles in clothing. While the men in their top hats discussed politics, travels and fox hunts.

The Dahl's church was made of old logs, had crude benches also made of logs to sit upon. There was a potbellied stove in the very middle of the room. Their faith seemed so different as well. Sometimes Rebecca wondered if the two churches were following the teachings of the same God. This small country church had a small congregation of worshipers who prayed out loud. The people usually had tears flowing down their weathered, but glowing faces. They had a rule to give 10% of even the tiniest amount of monies they earned to their church. Strange as the church services may have been to Rebecca, she soon learned to love these people and settled right into their way of believing. The faith, hope and belief they possessed was now exactly the belief system cherished by Rebecca.

Rebecca had agreed to raise her children in the same God fearing way that John believed. There were times she would question some of the things he and his church believed in. These things she could not understand, but followed the rules anyway. One thing she could never understand was their disbeliefs on anything that sparkled, or that of anything they considered to be vanity. She had removed all of her jewelry. Her pierced ear lobes that used to hold pretty earrings had long since grown back together after all of these years. The pretty low necked sparkling gowns in her closet had been taken down. They had been folded and placed into a big old trunk. Plus, she had placed other sparkling items in still a smaller trunk she had brought from New Orleans. These things were rarely even looked upon. They were hidden away in the upstairs. John's religion did not hold to wearing such things. The gowns were also viewed upon as vanity. Sometimes she felt as if she had traded in a life of beauty for one old church dress. That dress was made of very dark green velvet with an ivory lace collar and trimmed in wide ivory lace on the bottoms of the long sleeves. She also had three homemade sack dresses that she had tried to sew herself. These, she wore around the house. She was not trained in sewing, but had to learn fast once she became John Dahl's wife.

Amazingly, neither John nor his family had found anything incorrect about Rebecca's shoes. Therefore, holding onto the one thing she could from the past were her pretty, but now worn shoes. She also had a beautiful pearl purse no one seemed to complain about.    At times she would think of how silly she was for wearing high heeled lace-ups or button ups around the house and even in the fields.    She just told herself it was a necessity instead of vanity as John could not afford to buy her any new shoes.    She knew it was part of her past she did not have to give up and in spite of herself, she probably was holding onto a little vanity.    She did own too many pairs of shoes anyway.    They were however, getting old by now. John would nail little taps upon the heels and toes of these shoes as they became worn.

When wonderment thoughts would cross Rebecca's mind, she would often question how the way someone dressed had to do with their belief in God.    Did He really care how you dressed as long as it was in good taste and not as a harlot? Laughing at that thought she continued to walk along the path to the other field.    She made sure she was missing the cow patties along the way. The outside of these patties would harden by the sun, but if you made a mistake and stepped into one, you would sink and more than likely cover your shoes.    Believe me; it was surely wet on the inside.

As Rebecca reached the corn field, she placed the basket holding the sleeping baby under a large hickory nut tree and started to walk off. She then thought maybe she should not have done that.    She returned to see if there were any nuts on the tree.    Looking upward, she realized it must not be the season yet for the nuts to fall to the ground. So, she left James right where she put him.    She picked up a corn basket that was by the fence and headed towards the working children.    As she bent over to kiss Dale Henderson, her three year old,

49

she felt very dizzy. She realized she had not been in the sun long enough to be feeling this way. All of a sudden she felt a sinking feeling as a thought struck her like a bolt of lightning. Her mind was rattled with thoughts while thinking,

"Dear God, not again! James is too small. I do not want another child at this time. I am just tired."

John looked her in the eyes with a worried look, and then she smiled. He then threw her a kiss and said in that roaring voice,

"We and Me love you mother!"

Everyone went back to work at a steady pace. Everything was quiet except that noise made by the pulling off the shucks from the corn. This caused Rebecca's mind to wonder once again. As she started pulling off ears of corn, her mind went back to the day she had met that bronzed hunk of a man smiling down at her. She had often wondered by what miracle she had the right to have this gorgeous man's love. She thought of how she knew the very day she met him there would never be another man for her.

# C hapter 5

After Rebecca's studies at the university she had acquired a position at West Side Hospital. This hospital cared for many conditions, along with a very large unit that tended only to T.B. patients. Although only about ninety miles away from Aunt Amy's farm, she never got home much. Going home for visits had almost become unheard of. Letters had to make do. By then she and her sister had rented a one room efficiently apartment. The ladies tried not to over spend on anything. Every cent of money was still being used very sparingly by the sisters. They were busy putting more money away to assure each child would receive their education. Christmas seemed to be the hardest time of all during the time the sisters were still sharing living quarters. Some Christmas's they would find a small tree and just be thankful to have each other. This was a far cry from the ten foot trees resting in the corner of their large childhood parlor. But, they made do with what they had. They would always send small gifts home for the others.

Beatrice had met a nice young man who worked in the laboratory at the hospital. She was

51

counting what the girls felt would be her share of the additional amount of monies needed for Mary, Eva and Dale.  As soon as this accomplishment was reached, Bea hoped to be married.  This young gentleman had already ask her to marry him and she had accepted.  They had been engaged now for a good while.

From the letters they would receive from home, Eva was giving Aunt Amy fits.  She was only sixteen, but had a boyfriend.  Letters from Eva were full of excitement, but letters from Aunt Amy sounded worried.  Her young man was from a neighboring farm.  Eva was showing signs of believing an education was not all so important.  She didn't even want to finish High School.  Yes, she seemed hell bent on marrying this fellow.  Over and over again the girls had written her reminding her of their father's wish.  Aunt Amy was feeling she had failed in some way.  They tried to assure her it was not her fault.  Rebecca and Beatrice knew they should not leave this all for Aunt Amy to worry about.  They knew they should at least meet this young man before giving, or not giving approval of a marriage.  Even though their money was tight, they knew they must plan a trip home.  They each must ask for more hours at work or something to acquire the monies needed for the trip.

It came to pass Rebecca and Beatrice would go home shortly thereafter anyway.  They received a telegram one foggy August morning.  Their beloved Aunt Amy had passed away.  The telegram had stated she and Bea were expected to come home immediately to make funeral arrangements. Dale was a young man now. Mary was old enough to take care of herself and Eva was most surely going to marry her young man whether anyone objected or not. Rebecca still felt that it should of course depend on their approval of this young man. She thought maybe a marriage would not be so bad if Eva's young man would be of a help to Uncle Richard and Dale on the farm. The girls knew Uncle Richard, Eva and Dale were quite able to make the necessary planning; but they also knew Uncle Richard needed and wanted them there for support and appearances.

The ride back to Gallipolis, Ohio was not the nice trip Rebecca had enjoyed on the first train ride several years ago. Her mind kept going to the loss of yet another family member. She bit her lip to fight back her tears. Why was life so very short? Why were she, her sisters and brother meant to be so alone? Why did Aunt Amy have to die and leave that sweet, sweet man Uncle Richard alone? Not being blessed with children, maybe in some of heaven's planning that was why she and her siblings were sent to be in Southern Ohio.

Upon reaching the depot within the tiny city, Rebecca looked out the window to see the river on one side and the buildings on the other. The buildings stood so tall and majestic with their tall chimneys. Chimneys placed at each end of the big stores and the houses appeared very French, very French indeed. The stores had dressy awnings draped above their windows. What a beautiful little town. It reminded her so of her home New Orleans. There were many differences though. The leaves would soon be changing in color. The change would make this valley come alive with oranges, yellows and other beautiful colors. New Orleans stayed pretty much the same all year long. Both were very beautiful in different ways. She had learned to love the changing of the seasons. Fall season could not be matched by any other season for its beauty in Southern Ohio. Yes, she must have grown to truly be a buckeye, because she believed there was no prettier site than the rolling hills of Southern Ohio.

Rebecca realized upon arrival she had been homesick to see the valley. Gallipolis had an advantage over New Orleans. All of its stores faced the river. There was a large beautiful park right in the heart of town. Some rule had been placed to where nothing was to be built on the river side of the park. Someone had told Rebecca that it was so the beautiful Ohio River could be seen from all angles. She believed it was probably more because of the river trade. There was a tall gazebo in the very center of this park where bands would play on holidays and events. Usually the usage of this gingerbread covered gazebo was that of the politicians. The park employees or town's folks kept it so white and so pretty.

Rebecca stepped off the train at the Gallipolis Depot. She caught the hem of one of her petticoats on a nail which was sticking out from one of the rails. Somewhat embarrassed, she stepped to a bench to access the damage. She could feel eyes watching her. She looked up to see what she thought had to be some kind of a Greek God. The very first thing she noticed was curls, curls everywhere, blondish brown curls. She then seen the eyes that had to be the bluest she had ever seen. The sun light was making them dance. As those eyes twinkled and danced down at her, she felt she must have been frozen in time, because she could not pull her eyes away. Finally she somehow unlocked the stare and she moved her
54

eyes downward. She saw shoulders, large and solid that looked like carved rocks covered by the whitest shirt she had ever seen. The shirt had a very stiff stand up collar and garters holding up the long sleeves. They looked as if they were going to bust any minute from under the pressure of the strength of those bulging muscles. What was wrong with her? Never had she shown such un-lady like tendencies. She could not help it. She was letting her eyes drop even further as she saw those bulging muscles come perfectly down to a small neat flat stomach and tight waist.

Okay, this was getting to be very embarrassing. Rebecca removed her eyes and tried to act normal even though she knew her face had to be a bright pink and her knees were shaking. What happened to her speech? Why could she not at least say hello to this dashing young man? He just stood there with a big smile. Maybe it was a smirk instead, because he looked as if he was really enjoying her embarrassment. She looked back into his eyes to find him gazing into hers with a teasing look. He spoke in sort of a loud deep voice,

"Miss, may I be of any service?"
Now, Rebecca was sure she was very red because she could feel the heat on her face and neck. Somehow after much hesitation she was able to say,

"Yes! Why yes sir, you may bring that larger trunk over here to the bench if you please, and thank you for offering."
He moved towards the trunk with a great determination. She could not help but look at him even more while his back was turned. She almost

caught herself speaking her thoughts out loud when she thought,

"Lord, have mercy! What a picture of a man!"

The young man picked up the large trunk with ease and toted it over to where Rebecca was sitting.

"Thank You,"

she said once more. The next thing she knew he had sat down beside of her and he ask her name. She said with a squeak in her voice,

"Rebecca!"

It had to be those blue eyes she thought. If she would just not look at him then maybe she could come off as something other than a silly school girl. The young man told her his name was John.

"John H. Dahl"

he said with a big smile. He then started a conversation. She found he and his family lived and worked on a combination of farms of approximately 2,000 acres in the Northern part of Gallia County. The farms were maybe twenty miles from Gallipolis. He told her of how he had his heart set on purchasing about 50 acres. This was a plot with an old home on it. His family already owned the farm and he now worked it for himself. He got so excited while telling her of the hills and the forest on that farm. He told of how a creek runs right through the very middle of this pretty rolling hill farm. He told of how he could see the smoky steam flowing high above the trains on both their morning and evening runs through the valley, because the tracks were just over the back hill. His eyes got even brighter and bluer as he explained of how a prettier site one would never see. Rebecca found herself caught up in the conversation while he told her of how his life dream was to one day own this very special farm. John believed farming was in his blood and his desire was to be the very best of all farmers. He had ideas of an orchard beyond any orchard in the county. This young man definitely knew what he wanted out of life.

As John and Rebecca sat on that bench, time was passing by, but neither seemed to notice. It felt as if they had known each other forever. His dreams felt as if they were also hers right then and there. These were very strange feelings for someone with whom she had just met. Rebecca had become so lost in those blue eyes and this young man's dreams to where she had really forgotten Dale was to arrive to pick up her and her sister.

What happened to Beatrice anyway? Why had she left her alone to be so open to this stranger? Reality soaked in when she pulled herself away from those mystifying eyes long enough to see Dale walking down the platform. He had arrived to pick them up. She did come to her senses long enough to notice her brother was quite a man himself anymore. She hardly recognized him. He seemed taller and had more muscles and was larger shouldered than he was the last time she saw him. Although she hated the fact he had grown up so fast, she knew he too would make some young lady a very nice handsome catch.

Rebecca knew she must act like the lady she really was now and not be a bad influence to her younger brother. After all, the younger siblings were hers and Beatrice's responsibilities now. What would Dale think if he saw her flirting with

57

this young man? Bang! That thought struck home. Flirting, Wow! What a word! Is that what she was doing? Golly! She feared so. She looked further down the plank and realized Dale had driven that old farm wagon pulled by those two old worn out horses. She looked back to her brother and realized how handsome he was. She started to think of how father and mother never intended for him to be dressed like an old farmer or for his face to be so rugged and worn looking from the work load placed upon him. This made her sad for a moment. However, after all this family had been through this must have just been God's plan. Everyone seemed to have adjusted to their new lives quite well. Dale started waving and said,

"Hello Sis!"

He ran into Rebecca's open arms. At about that same time, Beatrice came walking along the planks with an ice-cream in one hand and swinging her purse in the other. She held her ice-cream high while she got a big hug from her brother. She then asked,

"Would you two like a soda or ice cream?"

At the same time Beatrice noticed the young gentleman standing there looking as if he was part of their party. So, she said,

"Hello Mr. whatever your name is."

He snapped right back quickly by saying,

"John H. Dahl madam, and to whom do I have the pleasure?"

Bea responded only after she saw the look on Rebecca's face by saying,

"Oh never mine me! I'm just her sister and my name is Beatrice, but you can call me Bea. And this is our brother Dale."

Dale reached out to shake John's hand and everyone seemed delighted to meet the other. John continued his involvement in their conversation by saying,

"I knew you two had to be sisters the minute I saw you together, as one does not see such beauty in many circles."

Then he said,

"Ladies, your carrier awaits you,"

as he was nodding at Dale. He was picking up that large trunk again. The next remark out of his mouth was,

"I am sure your brother does not appreciate you ladies talking with strangers, therefore I will leave the minute I get this young ladies full name and address."

He then looked at Rebecca and said,

"You can really get rid of me if you will tell me you will be at the fall-fest held in the park this following Saturday."

Rebecca then turned another shade of red. She quickly pulled a piece of paper from her purse and wrote down the information he requested. She then handed it to him. He folded it neatly and stuck it in his shirt pocket, then said,

"Thank you Miss Becky."

No one had ever called her that. Her father had called her Beck, but no one had ever called her Becky. She looked over her shoulder as she replied,

"Your fall-fest sounds wonderful, but I came home for a funeral and would not be in a mood; nor would it be proper for me to attend. But, thank you for inviting me."

This young man seemed to bring the teasing part of Beatrice out into the open. Just as they

59

were leaving, Bea looked up at the large young man and jokingly asked,

"Are you getting married today or something?"

She was looking at the black tie he was wearing. He replied in a teasing manner while showing a row of pearly white teeth,

"No madam, me (mum) has this firm belief that one should be clean and Godly. We Dahl's do not come to town dirty or without proper dress."

She then asked a question Rebecca had been too amazed to ask. That question was what he was doing in town. He told her he was there to deliver grain that would later be delivered to another city by the train. Rebecca could not help but notice Bea and John were conversing as if they were siblings or long lost friends. Dale also seemed to like this young man.

Waving goodbye to their handsome stranger, Bea and Rebecca climbed aboard the old farm buckboard. One sister got in on one side and one got in on the other side beside their brother while both kissed him on each cheek in the process.

"He-e-y Bea, did you notice the muscles and the dark tan on your handsome baby brother," remarked Rebecca. Bea screamed over a train whistle,

"Yeah, I sure did."

Dale looked embarrassed and remarked something about how he did not know how he had survived these months without their torture. All joking aside, they both noticed the child they had left behind had become a real man and a true farmer.

After a bout of teasing Rebecca for flirting with the handsome stranger, most of the trip to the farm was silent. They were all reflecting on the fact their beloved Aunt Amy had gone away. When they were getting closer to the farm, Dale told them that their cousin Chancy was coming as well. He planned on moving in with Uncle Richard, Dale, Eva and Mary. Grandmother had become less sufficient and could not care for herself anymore. Richard had begged her to come to live with them and had promised he and the children would take very good care of her. She refused as usual. She had planned for many years not to be a burden. She would say things like:

"I never want to be a burden to my children."

She was so determined to go to that old people's home! Rebecca felt badly about that, but knew she could not change the old woman's stubborn mind. She just wondered how she could ever go visit her. She also wondered just how long it would be before having to make this same trip for her grandmother's funeral.

The grandmother's house was to be sold and the monies given for her care. Aunt Amy had asked Uncle Richard to see that Chancy would get a share of their small farm when he passed. Aunt Amy felt it was unfair to Chancy that everything belonging to her mother had to go to the state for her care.

The next few days were busy and sad. Neighbors and friends of Aunt Amy and Uncle Richard brought food and stayed up all night at the house for a wake. The funeral was held in their small country church. Rebecca knew very few of the mourners, but appreciated each and every one who showed their respects. Poor Uncle Richard looked so lost. He just sat with his head down for

61

days and would eat or go to bed only after someone reminded him to do so. Dale was taking care of all the chores. She knew her Uncle Richard loved the children and thanked God they were there for him, but she also knew his life would never be the same without Aunt Amy. No one's would.

What was going to happen to Dale now? With the older girls gone he and Eva had taken on the responsibility of raising Mary, of course with the help of Aunt Amy and Uncle Richard. He would have to grow up even more to help with that farm. Eva was more than likely going to marry soon, then who would tend to the kitchen and the laundries. Mary was probably old enough but what about her youth? Would it go away and would she become a woman way too soon as her sister Eva had done?

While Bea and Rebecca were discussing all of this, they wondered about the educations. They knew Eva would surely not finish and Dale would have a hard time going to school. Mary would probably be the only one left who might get an education. With Aunt Amy gone there was no guarantee of that. Father would be so displeased with these ideas. Many of the discussions the sisters had on the train were worries unfounded. When they arrived at the farm they found these children had grown into very dependable and responsible young adults. What better to rob your childhood than the loss of one's parents, then the loss of a family member who cared for you the remainder of your youth?

Eva's young man was nice enough and not bad in the looks department either. Rebecca became concerned when he said something rather silly. This made Rebecca worry he was not ate up with a lot of intelligence, but she could see Eva was obviously taken up in adoring love for this man. Father would have never approved, but that was in another state, another life and another world.

Rebecca and Bea ask many questions of the younger siblings. They found Eva was not doing well in school. It was not from stupidity, she just honestly hated school. Dale told them he also had to keep her out of school a lot lately to help around the house. Aunt Amy had not felt good for a long time. Eva had been determined to marry her young man and forget about schooling. She did not understand why she needed any more schooling since she had no plans whatsoever to do anything but be a farmer's wife and raise beautiful children. So they all agreed she could get married, but made her promise she would educate herself further by the books each sister was going to send to her. It was decided the wedding was to take place within a proper time frame after Aunt Amy's burial, and with everyone's blessings.

Chancy's arrival happened just before the funeral. This gave him time to show his respect and regrets for his Aunt Amy, the woman who had cared enough to include him in his will. Though older than Rebecca and her siblings, he somehow looked younger. He was a very thin young man, looking as if he had never seen sunshine. Rebecca looked at him and surmised the rumors were most surely correct. Why the big secret? This young man had been so protected, but the looks and movements proved to her that Chancy had to be their brother. He just had too many characteristics like her father. Rebecca wondered if there could

63

be more to this story than met the eye since it seemed to be so hushed. Do you suppose her father and Chancy's mother weren't married or something? Well, she guesses if anyone wanted her to know the details then they would have surely told her. It was just a shame he had not grown up with his siblings and their father.

# Chapter 6

"Ouch!" That is the second time Rebecca cut her finger on a corn husk.

"Serves you right," she thought. She needed to keep her mind on her work. Remembering the past just made her more homesick to see her family. She had been thinking so much of all of them lately. Bea now had five children of her own and Rebecca had only seen three of them. How could she help but remember her past so often now with this deep need to see her family. It had been way too long since a visit.

She remembered leaving Aunt Amy's farm that fateful day after her aunt's death and arriving once again at the Gallipolis train depot. She was worn and had very swollen eyes. She was thinking of nothing but the loss of her wonderful aunt. She was so surprised to find Mr. Dahl once again at the train station. She wondered underneath her breath,

"Does he live here?" He smiled at her as she and Bea headed for the seating area. She looked into his eyes and once again she became concerned with the idea of whether her legs would carry her across the floor.

65

This man was most surely a danger to her health. She wondered if she was even walking straight and remembered the torn hem she had received at their first meeting. As Rebecca and Bea approached, John said,

"Hello ladies, I know this is not a good time for neither of you, but I wanted to wish you a safe trip home."

He then handed Rebecca a folded piece of paper. He had written his name and address upon this small piece of paper and ask her to write him. She then realized he more than likely was not delivering anything today, but was just there because one of them must have told him of the day they were returning.

Once again Rebecca noticed how neat this man was. His whole life must be perfect. Either that, or his mother was some kind of a clean fanatic. Maybe his clothes were made of some outer space material that does not wrinkle. Or he had stood up all day to look his best for her. That thought made her cheerful inside as she thought,

"Now that would be impressive!"

Then with a quick glance she realized it was just those muscles. His clothing had no room to wrinkle.

John smiled at her and she smiled back. Once again she could feel her face turning red. What was with her? She was an adult! She had always heard of chemistry, but she did not expect it to be the redness of one's face and neck. Rebecca knew John was enjoying every minute of her dismay. He walked up to her and exclaimed he had to come to Chillicothe, Ohio within three months to deliver some fruits to a market. He asked if there was any way she could meet him

66

there for a nice dinner and an evening on the town. At first she said no, while thinking there was no way she could afford another trip. Seeing the torn look on Rebecca's face, Bea leaned over and whispered,

"Remember? Eva is getting married. She doesn't need school money!"
Then as if it was another's voice, Rebecca heard herself say,

"Yes I would love to. I can rent a carriage for the day. Or better yet,"
she said with a smile,

"Why not another train ride? It is not supposed to be very many miles from Columbus to Chillicothe."
The date was set and arrangements were made to meet at the train station within that city. As he turned to walk away, John assured Bea and Rebecca they would not be unescorted. He would invite his sister Ethel to accompany them.

During the following months Rebecca wrote and received many letters. By this time it was as if she knew everything about this handsome, wonderful stranger. She also had poured her heart out to him while telling him everything about herself. They both must have fallen in love with each other the first day they met. Or, was it learning so much about this perfect man that had led her to believe she was already in love with him. Well, maybe it was just those beautiful blue eyes, the muscles or maybe that smile. She chuckled as she thought of how that would be sort of shallow, wouldn't one say? She giggled at her thoughts. Golly, who knows? All she knew was she wished she could spend the rest of her life just loving this man. Once more she giggled as she thought,

"What a career!"

Maybe Eva was right, what good would an education be if you turned into nothing but a farmer's wife?

Well, the months went by and Chillicothe turned out to be complete Heaven. In reality it was a stinking little town. It was a charming town with charming people, but stinky. There was a paper-mill there that had smells coming from it. If the wind was in your direction the smells would turn your stomach. Once you were inside somewhere you never noticed it. Besides, once Rebecca met up with John and met his sister; their presence made her forget the smells. The restaurant John had chosen was beautiful. The food was wonderful. Not until they were leaving did she remember the paper-mill. Once outside, ever so often the wind would pass by while bringing a smell similar to rotten tomatoes.

After dinner, John had suggested they go to a club of sorts where there was dancing. The place he chose was very similar to a ball room and this turned out to be great fun for all three. Rebecca found quickly that she adored John's sister Ethel. They were having so much fun. She realized John had not asked her to dance. She thought maybe he did not know how to dance. After all, he was always nowhere but on that farm unlike Rebecca who had come from both worlds. She also noticed he was drinking nothing but juice. Of course the ladies were doing the same. He also had said he felt sinful for being there, but wanted to take the ladies to somewhere they had never been just for the experience. He repeated over and over again of how their mother would never approve of such a place. With a bit of a worried look, he told of what he would tell his mother should she ever find out they were there. He said that he would tell her it was all Ethel's idea! Ethel then said,

"You liked the idea too, so you're not getting me into trouble. You're older and you are supposed to be in charge."

The beautiful evening passed. The night was spent in a rooming house. John's sister Ethel roomed with Rebecca. John got in a quick kiss on Rebecca's cheek as he walked the ladies to their room. Ethel and Rebecca really became acquainted that night. They stayed up to the wee hours of the morning. Ethel, still being a teenager and acting as most teenagers do, could not wait to tell Rebecca of how John would talk of nothing but her anymore. She informed Rebecca it was very obvious he was very much in love. She told Rebecca that their mother, brothers and sisters wished they would soon meet her. They wished John would just bring her home. She said this was so they could all get back to their normal lives and get some work out of John. Ethel told of how her family expected her to go back and report on how pretty Rebecca was and whether she liked her and so-on and so-on. Rebecca said,

"Well Ethel, my child what will you report young lady?"

The girls laughed. Ethel giggled and said,

"You pass! You pass with flying colors!"

They finally fell asleep. Rebecca returned to Columbus the following day. John and Ethel returned to Gallia County.

Rebecca would learn through later letters, the reason John had not ask her to dance. She had

69

become curious and written him to ask if he knew how to dance. She informed him in one of her letters that if he didn't, then she could teach him. He had written back and informed her that dancing was against their religion. She thought he was joking at first, so she wrote him back to say,

"John, after all it says in the bible to eat, drink and be merry!"

John assured her in his next letter that it was no joke. She shook it off with a funny thought of how much dancing one would do anyway on a fifty acre farm. She laughed about it and then forgot it. All she knew was she would be forever dancing in her heart from just one look into the confinements of those beautiful blue eyes.

Months passed, patients came and went at the hospital. Bea and her Lab Tech got married. They received word that Eva had also married. Their family was changing and getting bigger. John and Rebecca had made arrangements for Rebecca to come to a family reunion being held at his mother's home. It was to be three months after that night in Chillicothe. Rebecca had saved for the train trip. There had been no need for this though because John had sent her the money for the fare. This was such a nice gesture. She felt she should return the money though, as the trip had to be cancelled. John would not hear of this and ask that she buy something nice for herself instead. The hospital had fallen short of nursing staff and she could not take any time off. She was so disappointed, yet sort of relieved because she did not know how John's family would accept her. After learning so much about their beliefs, would John's family find her to be too worldly or too city like. What would she wear? How would she talk? How would she keep from being a nervous wreck?

A year had now passed. John and Rebecca were now writing letters about every day. If they lived closer, just think of the money they would have saved on postage alone. There seemed to be no doubt they were determined to be together somehow, someday. Christmas had come and gone and spring was approaching when Rebecca received a letter from John stating he must see her. He wrote that he had decided to leave the farm and move to Columbus to be near her. The bottom of the letter said,

"I will see you in one week".

Oh no! Rebecca did not want him to upset his life just for her. What had she done? No, he could not leave his beloved farm! Then it hit her that this letter was already a week old. She realized all of a sudden that the letter would have taken a full week to get there. It was now too late to talk to him first. He must be very close, even as she was reading his letter.

The next few hours were spent in a rush hunting clothes and shoes to wear while tidying up the apartment. What would she wear? Possibly she has been just a dream to this wonderful man? As much as she now loved him, would he later hate her for causing him to leave his farm dream? Would he still believe her to be beautiful? It had been a whole year. All of these thoughts ran around rapidly within her brain all night long and running rapidly into the next day. She now needed rest. She surely did not want big dark circles around her eyes when John arrived.

Two days had passed now and she had not heard from John. Her worries went from what to wear to worrying about him. It had now been two whole days without a letter. He was coming with horses and a wagon. Had he been given trouble along the way? It felt so strange not to receive a letter for two days. She knew he must stay some nights somewhere along the way. Where could he be? Then she told herself she would not worry. Everything had to be alright.

The evening of the second day, Rebecca had just lit the oil lamps when she heard a knock at the door.

"It must be John!"

She thought. Oh Lord her legs again! Why did they give out on her? She believed herself to be in such good health. How could John and she ever have a future if she could not get over the weak knee syndrome? She finally made it to the door, opening it just a crack to be sure of who was there. It was John! Now she knew she was going to fall down for sure. Her knees seemed to be knocking. Her hands were wet and she felt the need to go to the bath house, (Again)! For the last two or three days she believed she had gone at least one hundred times. Oh my, what did this man do to her!

Finally after what seemed forever Rebecca looked up into those dancing blue eyes. John was staring back at her. She was saying to herself,

"For God's sake, let him in!"

John just stood there with a big pearly white smile. He did say 'thank you' when she finally opened the door wider to wave him in. She remembered saying something like,

"It is good to see you!"

All she remembered afterwards was that he took her into his arms and held her so tight she wasn't

72

sure she could breathe anymore. He loosened his gripe enough to gently hold her. He then placed a long wonderful kiss upon her lips. She was sure the kiss lasted at least ten minutes.

"I shall surely faint,"

she thought during the long kiss. All the while she was thinking,

"Dear God, don't let him stop. Don't ever let him turn me loose."

John removed his lips ever so gently from hers and then he said,

"Rebecca, I love you! Being away from you has been the hardest thing I have ever done."

As he stood back away from her, he asked,

"Rebecca, will you please be my wife?"

Even though this is all she ever wanted, she was so surprised at this being the very first words out of John's mouth. He saw he had taken her by shock. He probably noticed this because of her lack of being able to speak. So, he joked with her by telling her,

"You have to marry me now Becky. One cannot kiss a lady like that without making an honest woman out of her."

It seemed like another ten minutes before she could get her mouth or throat or something to work. She tried so hard to say yes, but she had lost her voice. Then as fast as it went away it was back and the words seemed to flow like lightening. TOO LOUD, but her words did seem to come out a little less than a scream. She said,

"YES! YES! YES! Oh, YES! I will marry you!"

Things happened very fast after that. Rebecca was relieved to find that John had decided to come to Columbus for just one year. His plans were that he would get a job and save money to purchase that wonderful farm. He had already spoken with Beatrice about all of this. She had

73

told him he could live with her and her husband until their marriage. This disturbed Rebecca some while thinking of how the whole world must have known what was going on before she did. However, all of this made her so very happy! So, who really cared who knew first? The wedding was planned in a few months. John and Rebecca were to be married on Sunday, November 10th, 1907. They were to be married in a church on Highland Avenue right in the heart of the Hilltop, as people in Columbus, Ohio called that area. The hospital where Rebecca worked was also on the Hilltop. John had now acquired a position there as well. He was taking care of the horses and driving the head or official people of the hospital around. Wouldn't it be wonderful if mother and father could attend Rebecca's wedding? Times like this made her miss her parents even more. She knew she should count her blessings that Beatrice and her husband could be there. The other siblings would not be able to attend. This wedding was not to be the kind her parents would have planned in any stretch of the imagination. Neither was Beatrice's, nor Eva's. Eva's was just held in a living room.

John and Rebecca's wedding was to be very similar to Beatrice's. They were to have a few friends and co-workers in attendance and it was to be held in the church down on the corner. Rebecca could feel John's stress over his family not being able to come to their cherished wedding. They planned to take many pictures so everyone could see how wonderful the wedding would be. They were hoping this would lessen the stress of no one being able to attend.

# Chapter 7

The wedding took place as planned. Rebecca was a beautiful bride and John a very handsome husband. She wore a pale white crocheted dress that she had saved enough money in the past few months to purchase. It had a big 'V' in the front of the dress. It fit more like a jumper. She had purchased a very pretty silk blouse that had a two inch stand up collar and long puffy sleeves. There was about two inches of cuffs on the bottom of these sleeves that were made for the use of cuff links. She and Beatrice had believed this to be perfect since she had been given her mother's cameo that would fit very well in the middle of that collar. Beatrice had been given a pair of cuff links which also had cameo faces on them. It was wonderful to be wearing something that belonged to her mother and something that belonged to her sister. The cuff links worked as something borrowed. The beautiful lace dress flowed longer in the back than it did in the front. This caused the dress to drag the floor as she walked. She had borrowed still more petticoats from Bea making the dress very full and beautiful.

Rebecca could hardly remember what the Reverend had said during the ceremony. All she could see was her beloved husband. He looked more handsome than she had ever remembered him. His curls had been oiled down and combed to one side, making his hair seem darker. He had on a black tux with long tails and a wide collar on his shirt that stood up around that strong face. All she could do was to stare into those beautiful blue eyes. She knew this is where she would be safe and loved forever. Never in her life had she felt the happiness she felt on this very special and happy day.

John moved into the apartment with Rebecca after their marriage. There was no time for a honeymoon due to their work loads, but Rebecca would never forget that first night together. Beatrice had prepared a wonderful meal for the two of them and she had left it on the table ready for their return. The fire place was lit and she had candles ready to light everywhere. The Victrola was already cranked and ready to play. A soft record was laying aside. Everything was just perfect. Rebecca could not have been more pleased with her beautiful sister than she was right at that moment in time. She would never forget her wedding night. John had been ever so gentle with her. He kept asking her if he was hurting her. She had often wondered if he had even enjoyed that night because he seemed to be so worried about her. She knew she would never have to question his deep, deep love for her. As the nights moved into weeks the couple became more comfortable and more and more in love with each passing day.

The couple continued to work and save money until the day they were to move back to Gallia County. While counting their funds they realized they had fallen short of the purchase price of John's beloved farm. They were still determined to move as soon as possible. They had discussed staying in Columbus for another year, but neither really wanted to. So, they decided to get closer to home. This would give Rebecca a chance to visit with the rest of her family. It was decided to live in Racine, Ohio at Uncle Richard's farm until they could raise enough money to purchase their farm. John would leave Columbus a few months earlier than Rebecca so he could gather crops from the Dahl farms to sell at the farmers market. When he returned to pick her up he would bring the crops yielding along. He had also planned to sell his team and wagon when completing that trip. The couple could then travel home together on the train. John had felt traveling several days by horse and wagon may be okay for a man, but he refused to put his lovely wife through that kind of a trip.

It turned out that the farm John wanted so badly was not fifty acres as he had believed. It was only forty-six acres. They had a very good laugh about that one. Rebecca teased John by saying she would just have to plant her flowers closer to the house. Four acres may have been a nice planting patch or a pasture for some of the animals, but the couple took it all in stride. Not much could dampen their love or their happiness. They joked as to how they had lost four acres of land even before they purchased it. The two young people were now very close to the monies needed to purchase this farm. However, they

77

knew they would also need money to repair the old house and the run-down barns. John had told Rebecca of the two large barn's disarray. Now the plan was for Rebecca to turn in her work termination notice. She was however, to keep working until John could return. They would then stay at Uncle Richard's for a few weeks; or maybe even a month. During this time John would be gone a lot while helping with the Dahl's farms. Hopefully he would make enough money to purchase the property soon.

Things happened very fast after that. In actuality it was about three months, but time moved pretty fast because there was so much to do. Rebecca occupied her time by training new staff at the hospital, packing and making arrangements. The newly wedded couple missed each other very much, but they both knew they were working towards their brighter future. Deep inside of their hearts they knew once this time was over they would never be apart again.

It came to pass grandmother's house was empty. The government was willing to rent it to John and Rebecca. The rent monies were small, but it still felt as if they would be taking monies from their saved farm purchase money. It was taking more time to get that money needed for the purchase of their farm. More than either had believed. Though welcomed with open arms, the two felt they could no longer impose on Uncle Richard. So, Rebecca took a job working with the sick around the Racine area for very little money. John worked anywhere he could to make money and they moved into the grandmother's house.

After still another two years of saving money while loving one another more every day, taking long walks in the parks or just working long hours; John and Rebecca had become three. They became parents to a sweet little daughter they named Elizabeth. She was a beautiful little doll baby. She looked somewhat more like a boy in Rebecca's eyes. This was because she had inherited her father's broad face and his blonde curls. As she grew and her hair became longer, she became daintier, more beautiful and looking like nothing but a little girl. Eva, who now had a small son, could not keep her hands off of Elizabeth. This made it very handy for Rebecca because she could leave Elizabeth with Eva while she worked.

The days spent near Aunt Amy's farm were very nice. Chancy had become a strong young man. Uncle Richard, who was now aging, got down in his back often. He often said he did not know what he would do if it were not for Dale and Chancy. As for Chancy, a little farming and a little sun was all he needed. Rebecca was so proud of these two young men; 'Her brothers'! Yes, she knew she could now say that Chancy was truly a brother. She had two brothers now. Neither would ever go on to a higher education, but both were very resourceful and both knew how to make good money from farming. They were just like two peas in a pod. It was very easy to see they loved one another and were proud to be brothers. Rebecca did not know why her parents or other family members had waited so long to tell any of the children the truth about their brother. Chancy had always known, or at least grandmother had told him somewhere along the way. It seemed even Chancy had been advised to keep this twisted skeleton in their closet, only admitting to the truth after complete pressure from all of the siblings. It seemed strange that it had remained in the closet even if everyone knew in their hearts the rumor was very true. One's guess was that the full facts of this secret would never be told.

Finally, the day arrived when John and Rebecca felt they had saved enough money to begin their new life on their very own farm. John had missed farming very much. He had tried not to let it show to Rebecca. He knew she was more of a city girl by now. However, Rebecca had been very happy to come home to show off John to her family. She was also so very happy to be there at the birth of Elizabeth. She needed her family so much at that time. Within the next week, Beatrice and her family were to come from Columbus for a visit. Bea at that time had two children and the whole family was going to have a reunion of sorts before John and Rebecca moved.

After about three days Rebecca could see John was growing impatient to get to their new farm. He would not say anything, but Rebecca knew she should explain they would be leaving on Sunday. This was the same day someone was to take Robert, Bea and the children back to the train station. Dale had volunteered to do this, but Rebecca felt she should volunteer to take them on their way to their new farm. This would give John the opportunity to escape her family without being begged to stay for just one more day, as was so often done.

Although the new property was only thirty or forty miles away, Rebecca was concerned over the traveling by horse and buggy with a baby. They now had planned their trip to correspond with the trip back to Columbus for Robert and

Beatrice. Rebecca's thinking behind this was to kill two birds with one stone as one would say. They could deliver the other family to the train station and John would be well on his way to the new farm ownership. Rebecca did not want to let Beatrice go before she had to anyway, so she loved this idea.

Once they arrived in Gallipolis, Ohio, John told Robert, Bea and Rebecca that he had made arrangements with his family to leave a large wagon and team of horses at the stables. He was to pick them up for his and Rebecca's trip. The little buggy would fit upon the wagon and the two horses the men had ridden could walk along beside. This would be safer and have much more room for the trip. The luggage and the boxes of belongings now cramped up over the wheels of the buggy and the ones tied onto the back of the horses would find enough room in the wagon. Elizabeth could also have a nice little bed in the form of a basket for her trip.

The ladies and children were to stay at the station while John and Robert went to the stables nearby to pick up the team and wagon. Robert kept remarking of how this was such a beautiful town. Bea informed him he should someday see New Orleans if he believed this town to be so beautiful. The ladies just sat there quietly enjoying each other's company, yet knowing they would soon have to part. Bea placed her hand upon Rebecca's. Upon the men's return, time had come to say goodbye to her beloved sister and family. Rebecca cried, then Beatrice cried and the men started believing now that maybe they should have made other plans because the tears just seemed to not stop. The girls would hug. Then

81

they would cry, then hug again and cry again. Robert and John both realized how hard it was for the two ladies to say goodbye without knowing how soon they may see each other again.

The train pulled out of the station heading for Columbus, Ohio in the late afternoon. Rebecca waved until it was out of site. It had taken all morning of traveling to arrive at the station and then several more hours before the train arrived. John and Rebecca had another twenty miles to go and it was already getting dark. Rebecca knew they should be moving on. John reached down and put his arms around Rebecca and told her they would someday go to Columbus to visit with Robert and Beatrice. He said Robert and Beatrice would surely also return on visits. He told her of how she should be happy they were able to spend so much time together this time. She knew he was just trying to comfort her, so she reached over and clamped her hand around his. She thanked him for being so kind and they started off towards beginning their new life.

As they were pulling away from Gallipolis with all of its gas lights flickering they were slowly pulling into the darkness of the country side, Rebecca tried to console herself. She could not do much for herself as she was just remembering of how hard it was to say goodbye to everyone. Bea and Rebecca had been each other's best friends forever. Now letters were going to have to be their only contact until only God knows when. In her heart she did know they would at least get to see each other through the years of their lives, but also knew those visits would probably be very far and in-between. Unlike the olden days when so many went west. Those

82

families had to know when they left each other they were never going to see each other again. Thank God, her family may be strung out, but other than distant cousins and other loving people like those in New Orleans, her close family members were all close enough to see each other once in a while.

John and Rebecca were well on their start towards their farm now. It seemed as though the trip was taking forever. The trip from Racine to Gallipolis had not been a short one either. But the trip from Gallipolis to the Dahl world seemed like it would never end. Rebecca also knew once they were settled in or possibly as soon as they arrived she was going to meet the whole Dahl family. To this date she had only met Ethel. She was looking forward to knowing everyone, yet she was very nervous about the whole thing. She just hoped everyone would like her.

John took so many turns. Rebecca prayed she would never have to find her way back by herself. She would surely be lost. The likelihood of that would be very rare however because women did not travel alone. It was getting very dark now and Elizabeth had awakened so Rebecca took her into her lap. In a short time the precious baby was once again asleep. John was very quiet. You could hear the heavy foot prints made by the horses. You could hear the squeaks, squeaks and more squeaks as the wagon would make those noises with each turn of the wheels. After climbing a couple of pretty big hills, Rebecca noticed that John was steering the horses into a small lane of sorts. There were two ruts and grass growing tall between them. The weeds were brushing along the bottom of the wagon. Even in

83

the dark Rebecca could see John's bright smile with his pretty white teeth. He turned to her and said,

"This is it Darling! This is our home!"
John jumped off the wagon and asked Rebecca to stay put while he took the lantern and prepared them a place to sleep. With a nervous laughter he informed her that tomorrow at sunbreak he would at least make one room livable. Then she could hear him talk to himself not meaning for her to hear, when he said,

"Gosh, this place looks worse than I thought."
As he walked along with the lantern burning brightly, Rebecca was viewing every spot she could see. The minute John got out of site; she could feel hot tears running down her face. From what she could see through the darkness, the house had broken windows. One whole side of the house had fallen in. She stared in wonderment as she wondered what was that in what looked like the parlor?

"Oh dear God, that is a tree!"
A tree had grown up inside the house and right through the roof. Rebecca knew she was not to get down doing any investigating because the weeds were as high as the wagon. What about creatures? Curly furry creatures? She could hear John returning and she felt ashamed of her feelings. This was John's dream. Thank God it was dark and he could not see her crying. She wiped her tears with her sleeve as he stepped back upon the wagon. He said,

"I'm sorry honey, this has changed so much since I last seen it. I must have been thinking of a different season. One without all this growth. We cannot stay in there tonight. I will make us a bed in the wagon."

Rebecca felt great relief come all over her.

The next morning John, with the help of his family, put on a new roof. As promised they cleaned, painted and fixed one bedroom for the family to sleep in. They had to walk across planks to get to that room, but it was nice and free of all creatures. All weeds and debris had been removed which made Rebecca feel so much safer.

John's mother had given them a really nice bedroom suit. The one John had always slept in. The handles on the dresser and the chest looked like wings craved out of wood. There were a few glass swinging handles too, and the headboard was very pretty. It stood tall and had wood carvings with what looked like big wings or leaves going out from the middle. The mattress was of the softest feather bed she had ever slept upon. Her mother-in-law had also furnished them with a big pretty wool rug that covered the biggest part of the room and some pretty lace curtains. This one room had turned out to be lovely, quite lovely indeed.

Rebecca fell in love with her new family immediately. The Dahl family was so kind and so happy to meet Rebecca. For each meal, John and Rebecca went to the adjoining farm to his mothers, her mother-in-laws to eat. This became a way of life until they finally fixed up a kitchen. The new mother-in-law loved Rebecca and was completely fascinated with the granddaughter. She wanted to keep Elizabeth constantly.

During the following years, the other children were born. The house was repaired room by room and a new kitchen was added at a later date. John then made, what had been the temporary kitchen into a very nice seating room. It was hard to believe that old house was over one hundred years old when they purchased it. It had nearly fallen down. Now the growing Dahl family lived, laughed and grew up in the happy old house that had looked so sad in the dust of night. It had now become a home and a very pretty home place indeed.

Rebecca had no idea John was such a carpenter. He had fixed and added many extras to make this home what it had become. The new porches now had ginger bread trim and the main front porch had a big nice swing. By now they had purchased some items. They had returned a couple of times to Aunt Amy's farm to collect some furniture the children had brought with them from New Orleans. Rebecca had decorated a corner for her mother's beautiful organ. The one she had purchased for her mother's birthday so long ago. It had been a used organ when she purchased it. It had come from their church because their church was buying a new one. When she arrived at the farm she found her sister Mary had taken much interest in playing it, therefore she did not have the heart to take it away. Instead she told Mary to take it with her on the day she moved into her own home and that she could use it just as long as she wanted to.

Uncle Richard had all of grandmother's belongings packed away here and there. Though he said it in the nicest way, he insinuated his mother-in-law was a pack rat. He then stated of how he would be most appreciative if some of the siblings would take some of these belongings off his hands. Grandmother had been a bit of a saver or clutter type person.  So, John and Rebecca had brought many items to their farm that the other siblings had not claimed.  By now they had moved two really good size wagons.  The other married children had taken bunches too.  With all this furniture and household goods, along with those items given to them by the Dahl's, the young couple had quite an upstanding looking home. Rebecca even got a piano from one of John's sisters.  She placed it in that corner she had prepared for her organ and she was now learning to play.  She could play a few old southern songs. Both she and John felt their home was quite beautiful. Who would have ever believed they could do so much with that old place.  John's dreams had come true and so had Rebecca's.  She had a beautiful home, precious children and a loving, wonderful husband.

Rebecca was not a good seamstress, but good enough after trial and error to make some pretty curtains throughout the house.  As mattresses would go flat, the Dahl family had killed enough chickens or raised enough crops to have plenty of feathers and straw to fill the pillows and mattresses.  Mrs. Dahl had taught Rebecca how to really cook and was working on her sewing techniques each day.  She would show her how to can foods and store meats.  All the things someone else had done for the family in Rebecca's youth. She had learned much during her stay with Aunt Amy, but was still lacking in so many departments.  She was very pleased someone would take the time and interest to train her such things.  Her mother-in-law would laugh when Rebecca would become all mushy with 'Thank Yous'! She would say,

87

"Girl, do you think I want my family to starve or go naked?"

The jolly old lady had lost her husband years ago, but had stayed strong and raised her children who now tried really hard to take care of her. Brother-in-law Andy, from down the road on the other side, had said she was an impossible ole' woman and God help them all when she really would get sick. They would have to hog tie her to keep her still. Rebecca just laughed and thought of how lucky she was to have such a wonderful mother-in-law. She could see where so much of the kindness in John had come from his mother.

Over the years, Rebecca had planted flowers all along the garden fence. One beautiful big yellow flower bloomed all the time and climbed up over the rounded gate that opened into the garden. At the one end of the very large garden the family had planted a full raspberry patch. Along the end of that fence grew what was called goose berries. On the other side of that fence was the most fragrant lilac bush. Wisteria was draped all over the end of the kitchen. Fruit trees had been planted about the large yard and John had planted that perfect orchard. They had re-built the two barns and added several sheds. They had built two corn cribs. Blackberries grew all up and down that bank by the new long chicken house. They were the proud owners of several cattle, lots of chickens and a few pigs. They owned a team of work horses and a couple quarter horses. Rebecca was partial to the one they had named Prince. They had acquired many pieces of equipment and had made themselves a very nice, sometimes profitable farm. Well, one might say profitable, but what was meant was it was a very self-sufficient farm that met all of their needs.

Each spring, berries were everywhere. The gardens grew full. This fed the family fresh fruits and vegetables throughout the summer. In the fall, it was the time for canning season. Rebecca and the bigger children canned hundreds of jars of beans, peaches and other foods. They used a lot of big gallon stone jars. These jars had a little tin lid that sealed with hot sealing wax. The wax was red. When they purchased the property there was already a cellar on it, but John had built a smoke house up over that cellar. The canned goods were kept in the cellar. Potatoes were dug and placed in what was called a potato bin, also in the cellar. The cellar was cool in the summer and warm in the winter. Meats were kept upstairs in the smoke house after being smoked and salted. These meats would hang from the ceiling.

The children got real excited when they would make sauerkraut. They usually ate too much of it during the processing to where most everyone was sick at the stomach the next day. But for some reason this was an exciting time of the year. They would borrow a cabbage cutter from John's brother Andy. It was about three feet long and with a deep wooden tray that had three sharp blades in the bottom. You would put that across a barrel or a big stone jar and cut the cabbage. Then Rebecca would put a lot of heavy rock like salt on it. She had a big square blade with a long handle on it which she would chop up and down the barrel to be sure it was all finely cut. She would then weigh it down and cover it. This would make it good for all winter. The course salt came in a big sack. About twenty-five pound bags. This course salt was used for everything from giving to cows to being used on the kitchen table. The family never had fine salt.

When the pickles were ready to pick, Rebecca and the children would put water in a five gallon jar. They would put a lot of salt in it. The rule was to put in enough salt to float an egg. Then they would clean the pickles and put some into the brine as it was now called. These pickles were called summer, or bread and butter pickles. They lasted a long time and were very good on homemade bread with homemade butter.

The family would lay big sheets of fabric over the concrete patio John had placed at the back of the home. This was the process used to dry fruits. They would slice and lay out one piece at a time to dry in the sunlight. This was the family's source of sweets during the long winters. The fall was the season for butchering the beef and a pig. They had carefully fed the ones to be butchered all summer to get them to the perfect tenderness. Each fall a really poor old fellow from down the road a few miles would come to help butcher. He wanted all the parts the family did not use. John would always throw in a few steaks as well. Some of the meat was canned for different reasons, but most was smoked, salted or sugared and placed into the smoke house to be cured.

Farming was hard work, but with the training Rebecca had received while at her aunt and uncles and from her new family, she was now pretty good at it. She could milk a cow at 5:00 in the morning, have breakfast on the table, and have at least four children washed up and ready for school by 6:30 a.m. All the children would mock in a joking way behind her back of course at what

their mother had started the habit of saying each
and every morning. Those shoes she owned as a
young woman must have been made of the very
finest of leather because they still were quite
comfortable and still quite wearable. Her fine
shoes with the taps upon them would hit that
concrete patio in a run after she had milked the
cows. You could hear the click-e-d-clack as she
approached the house. She would walk in an
almost run and she would always scream,
"Everybody up, you're BURNING SUNSHINE!"
Each child knew they had better jump out of bed,
get dressed and tend to their chores.

# C hapter 8

Along about the 1920's, people on the surrounding farms were purchasing cars. John had his heart set on a Model T Ford but felt he may have to settle for a Model A. The buggy roads were so narrow and the winters in Ohio took its toll on the mud filled ruts or ditches they called roads. Now with cars the ruts were getting deeper and deeper until the roads were many times impassable. Rebecca's pretty buggy was tucked away in a shed type garage and had not been used in years. She had long since put her side saddle up as well. Times were changing and raising a family had taken its bite out of her desires to travel anywhere.

Rebecca had received letters from her sisters, Beatrice and Mary who both lived in Columbus now. She wrote back to them often. She, Chancy, Dale and Eva were the ones who stayed down in the woods. The saying "down in the woods" seemed to be invented by Mary. She would say that every time she would leave her job of teaching to come to the southern part of Ohio. Letters were filled with thrills while the girl's letters had told of how the roaring twenties were

93

really exciting. The 1920's were thought of as being a time of exuberance, hedonism, and prosperity in contrast to the hardship of World War I. Some magazine editor had taken bunches of pictures of a club and had titled his story the 'Roaring Twenties'. It took hold and everyone was calling these years the (Roaring Twenties)!

Beatrice had shipped her Victrola to Rebecca by train a few weeks past. She had included a few records that were now very popular. Robert had purchased Beatrice a new, more modern music player for their anniversary. Bea knew how much Rebecca missed having music around. So, she sent the old one to her sister. While cranking the machine, Rebecca could feel the excitement build up inside of her. The music was very up-beat and very crazy. Crazy, yes that was the word, crazy wonderful new music. She must share this with the children.

Rebecca and the children would listen to the new records while John was out in the fields. She was not quite sure how he would approve of such wild and gay things. She knew Beatrice, who still attended such a church as they had attended while living in New Orleans felt it was wonderful music for her children to listen to and to dance to. She told in her letters of how she and Robert had even been to a couple of Speakeasies. Rebecca and John on the other hand only allowed their children the church outings and those things which one could consider Godly. Oh, Rebecca was not complaining. She just wished her children could get a little more culture out of life.

Rebecca had indeed been in the early stages of being pregnant that fall day when she was so concerned while in the corn field. On March 17,

1924, she gave birth to another beautiful little girl. They named her Edith Bea. Naming her after two beloved sisters from both sides of the family. The Dahl's now had eight children. They had four boys and four girls. A nice even number Rebecca had often thought and she had hoped to stop at that. But on August the 13th, 1926 she had still another little girl. They named Mary Bella. Each child was so unique in their own right. They were all lively, beautiful children who worked hard, played hard and grew up beautifully.

Elizabeth, in her twentieth year during 1928 had introduced to her family a nice dark headed young man from the neighboring village of Vinton. She, her sister Gwen, the oldest son John Jr. and the following son Everett had taken an old buggy to school in Vinton all of their high school years. The older children had made this trip for years now while also hauling their cousins who lived nearby. The grade school children still went to the Bunker Hill School. This was a little one room schoolhouse for the grades one through eight. The grade school was down a hill in front of the house and then up another large hill. It was about two miles away. John and Rebecca had taught each child he or she were responsible for the younger children. This had worked very well. Their children were very well behaved and respectful towards each other. Rebecca felt so sorry for the younger children who had to walk to school. They had to go whether it rained, sleeted or snowed.

Elizabeth and some of the children from the village of Vinton had now gone on to the Rio Grande College. This college was several more miles away. Elizabeth had started her higher

95

education three years before. By the beginning of the school year in 1929, she had only one more year to go. John Jr., who was second born, had also been attending that college for the past year. Gwen, who was third born, had one more year of high school and would be in her first year of college the following year. Elizabeth wanted to be a school teacher. John Jr. just wanted to learn how to increase production of the farm. Gwen had decided to follow in her mother's footsteps and become a nurse. The Rio Grande College now had courses that would be real beneficial to all. This certainly made John and Rebecca happy because their children could get an education without running off to Columbus, Ohio in the same way Rebecca and her sister Beatrice had to do for the education they received. These parents knew they could have never afforded to send each of their children to a higher education had they taken off to another school. The Rio Grande College enabled each of them to come home evenings and to work on the farm to help grow the products that would pay for their tuitions.

Rebecca was sure Elizabeth and her young friend had become closer friends while making their trips on an old bus that run from Vinton to Rio Grande. Of course they were already a couple while in high school. The two were now talking about marriage. John and Rebecca had insisted they wait until Elizabeth graduated college. They had hoped she would secure a teaching position before such plans were made. In order to acquire such a position Elizabeth would need to complete all four years of her schooling. John and Rebecca had now met with the other parents. Both sets of parents decided this was of the most importance.

96

The younger people had agreed to wait until after graduation upon their parent's request.

In the next couple of years life went on as usual. Elizabeth did not get married the minute she got out of school and that made everyone happy. She interned as a teacher at the school in Vinton to better her knowledge and be close to her fiancé. John Jr., who only took a two year class, was telling his father of how to better their gardens and orchard. He told of how to plant crops in boxes instead of flat in the soil. His father would often just look at him and say,

"I spent good money for you to go to school to learn those kinds of things?"
He then would say,

"I've been farming since I was two and I think I should know a little morsel about it."

The respect the children had for their parents kept John, Jr. from arguing his point. Never-the-less his father did give him a large corner of the house garden to try his experiments in. To everyone's amazement, his box gardens did very well and were easier to keep weeded. However, this was not a plan for a large garden. One could not tend to a very large space on his hands and knees, so John Jr. only tried the boxes that one year.

John did get that Model T. However, John Jr. drove it most of the time. The dirt roads were so bad certain times of the year to where the car became useless. The Dahl's would pile the large family into the car to go to church every chance they got. Rebecca was always worried John would kill the car on the hills. So she would make the bigger children get out and walk up the inclines. The little ones never had to get out. James George often took advantage of his place in line of being the seventh child and would often play opossum to avoid the long trek up the hills. John and Rebecca knew he was doing this, but thought it was sort of cute and left him alone. He was still young in age even though his size would put him a year or two older.

All of the children got along with each other very well. There simply was not any time for meanness. Each child had many chores to do. Rebecca really enjoyed the youngest three. She knew she enjoyed each one before that, but believed these would be the last. She hoped that to be true anyway, and wanted their years to count. James was a stocky little guy who grew taller than the other boys had at his age. Not just taller, he looked like a little shrunk down man. His shoulders were very board and he seemed to have muscles at a very early age. He just grew and grew. He was a strong little fellow as well. He would pull his younger sisters up and down the hills on wagons, wood boards or shovels in dry or snowy weather.

Bella and Edith would play dress up and sit in the old white buggy for hours on end. Some days they would have James gather them all sorts of left over household goods so they could build a play house. They loved their brother James George and allowed him to join in as the father of their little make-believe house. All three would make mud pies and needless to say at the end of the day especially if it was a summer day, Rebecca was more than happy to have them bathe in the wash tub outside. She would fill the tub with the help of one of the older children early morning and the sun would heat the water. This made the perfect bath. The children loved it so much. It was all she could do to get them out of the tub and to get them to go to bed.

On winter days the smaller children followed the older children's habits by going upstairs and rumbling through old clothes, old papers or Sunday school cards that Rebecca had stored in the trunks. They seemed to like just lying on the straw filled beds and listening to it rain on the tin roof on rainy days. Winter night baths were given to the children while each stood on a wrap-around bench behind a potbellied stove. Once they were dressed in their warm pajamas or gowns, they would then hold their blankets up to the stove to get them warm. They would wrap themselves in their nice warm blankets and then they would immediately run up the steps to the chilly upstairs. While keeping wrapped in their warm blankets they jumped straight into bed. Yes, John and Rebecca were truly blessed to have such loving children and such a wonderful family.

Christmas was a very happy time. One year Rebecca was able to have her whole family come to visit. She felt that was the happiest Christmas of all. The cousins all had so much fun together. Uncle Richard had passed away the year before. Everyone had not been able to come to his funeral. So, they all felt this get together was very important. Dale had married. He and his wife had lost a set of twins in childbirth. This had been sad for everyone. Mary had gone on to school with the last bit of school money. She had become a school teacher. There was some talk she may be interested in marrying a certain young man instead of being an old maid school teacher. Chancy had so often teased her by calling her that.

99

One thing about Rebecca's siblings, they sure knew how to joke and tease with each other. This is probably one reason they enjoyed each other's company so very much. Chancy had also married a very sweet young lady named Majel. Rebecca thought of how they all liked her long before they ever met her because of her name being so similar to their beloved Mabel. She had a very funny accent though and everyone got such a charge when they would hear her say,

"Cha-n-cy start the machine,"
in a funny sounding lingo.

Actually this sounded very dignified, as she was more recently from Europe. The Dahl's called a car a car, but Majel called it a machine. She and Chancy sure had a pretty one too. It had a drop top with a rumble seat hanging over the trunk. Chancy would take the children for rides in it and they all always wanted to ride in the rumble seat. Chancy would crank while Majel would start the car/machine. Strange, how easy it was to entertain that Dahl bunch of children. Rebecca loved seeing them have fun. Her brother Chancy, who now lived in Gallia County, came to visit more often than those who lived in Columbus. He had not started a family yet so he was really involved with Rebecca's children. Everyone got so excited when he and Majel arrived for a visit.

On Christmas there was no fireplace to place stockings upon, just a couple old potbellied stoves and the kitchen cook stove. So, the children would put one of their shoes under the tree. John and Rebecca would place an orange, candy and nuts in a bag and stick them into the shoes. Before that day there was of course the gathering of the tree. This was always very exciting. They often had to go way back into the woods to find just the right size. John would hookup the horses and wagon, gather up all the children from the largest to the smallest and stay gone a big part of the day. The bright eyed children would search for him a tree to cut down. This was always a very special occasion for John and the children. Rebecca would bundle them up and fix hot chocolate for them to take along Always hot chocolate, now a tradition. The stone jar kept the hot chocolate warm for a big part of the day. Once they had the tree they wanted they would start back towards the house while singing Christmas carols.

Once the tree got back to the house, John would cut on it until it was just the perfect size. Then he would stand it in a corner. Rebecca would start the Victrola and put on a Christmas record. The family would then string popcorn and berries to hang upon that tree. Rebecca would bake ginger bread men. Actually she would make the dough and the children would cut out the shapes. Every year they would end up with some really different shaped ginger bread men. Some resembled more of a clump or something. Who cared, once they were iced, they still looked great upon the tree. This was always much fun and the house was filled with much joy and laugher.

The family did have a few ornaments. Rebecca had saved some from her childhood and John's mother had given them any that were important to John when he was a child. John, being the carpenter that he was and being so good with his hands, would make the smaller boys little wooden cars or planes. They would have wheels that really worked. Rebecca would make rag dolls for the girls. Occasionally she would buy a porcelain doll face and hands and make a really special, pretty doll. This was usually done when she knew that would be the last doll an older girl would want. Other gifts were clothing items that the children needed. Many of these items Rebecca had hidden in a corner of her bedroom and had sometimes sewn on them for months.

Winter days seemed so short and were spent doing chores. It seemed once breakfast was over it was time to start lunch. The afternoon was filled with baking bread, churning butter or making cottage cheese. Then it was time for dinner. By the time dishes were done there was the tending to the children's needs and any mending that had to be done. Laundry took all day at least one day a week. John had recently purchased a crank washing machine. The only problem with this new machine was that the day after a washing Rebecca could hardly move her right arm. She would have pains because of all that heavy cranking. Often the older girls would take turns with the crank. It was still so much nicer than scrubbing all day on a wash board. The wash board hurt shoulders no matter how you did it. Rebecca thought this new machine was wonderful because she had been washing her clothes on a washboard all of her grown up life. She had to laugh at her long past thoughts of her younger days. She now used that dreaded lye soap that she was so worried about when she arrived to this part of the country. She now even knew how to make it. Contrary to all of her first beliefs, she found it could be used for just about everything. She laughed as she thought of how it really was not bad for one's hair either.

On one winter morning Rebecca lost her mother-in-law.  She just did not wake up one morning and went to meet her loved ones on the other side.  John and the children took her death very badly and her beloved sister-in-law was torn for months.  Her mother-in-law had taught her so much and was so missed by everyone since her death.  Rebecca had really loved this sweet little old lady from the very first day of years ago when she had first met her.  It was as if she had now lost two mothers.  It was a very sad time for all.  The late Mrs. Dahl had lived a nice long life and had devoted all those years to her children.  John's sister Ethel had been married several years before her mother's death.  They stayed with the mother.  She and her husband were now John and Rebecca's permanent next door neighbors.  They had now purchased grandmother's farm from the other children, securing their home for the rest of their days.  Ethel now had five children who played with John and Rebecca's children every chance they got.  During these years your closest neighbor was at least one to two miles up or down the road.  So the visits were not on a daily basis.

In the spring of 1931, Gwen graduated nursing school. She seemed to be the most talented of the older children.  Unlike Elizabeth with her blonde curls and board strong face, Gwen was of smaller features and had very dark hair.  Sometimes when it shined in the light it looked almost black.  She had graduated from High School at seventeen and was now graduating nursing school at nineteen.  Each child was so unique in their very own way to where Rebecca often wondered how they could even be brothers and sisters.  Each was their own little soul with

103

their own little desires.  Gwen wrote poetry and read books all of the time.

Just before Gwen graduated from High School she had spent all summer that year looking for butterflies that had passed away recently.  This project was for the three middle children Everett, who was next younger than she; Mabel who was two years younger than Everett and Dale Henderson who was two years younger than she. They needed a science project the following year for school and the teachers had assigned the projects so each team could be of family groupings. This gave them time to finish their projects during their summer months, even if they were not in the same class.  The butterflies were Gwen's idea.  They could have chosen almost any kind of insect, but Gwen felt the butterflies were the most beautiful.  Rebecca believed towards the end of the summer Gwen was pretty sorry she had talked her siblings into this particular project.  She had too big of a heart to kill a butterfly or to kill anything for that matter.  She had to hunt constantly to find one that had just died or one that was caught in a spider's web.  She would painstakingly remove each little wing from the clutches of a web.  She would dry off their tiny wings if one had fallen into the water or was stuck in the mud.  She would feel sorrow because they had died in such a way.

One of Ethel's boys, full of mischief, was always thinking of some easier way to do things. Just last fall he had gone around with an old wooden wagon stopping at every local farm.  He was going from farm to farm selling a bushel basket full of corn cobs. He told his customers the corn cobs were good for starting fires and for
104

personal uses. To everyone's surprise, he was getting a nickel a basket. It amazed Ethel and Rebecca as to how many people actually purchased these baskets from him. It just showed just how resilient this little lad was. One just never knew what he would come up with next. Since he braved off of his farm every chance he got, he spent a lot of time with the cousin bunch of children. Gwen had to keep a very close eye on him that summer. She felt he often had killed some of the butterflies that he would bring to her. She suspected him because he was finding way more butterflies than anyone else. When she felt they had enough, she was happy to close the project. The children got busy and glued each pretty butterfly to a pretty paper. They then framed their work in a large glassed frame that Elizabeth had purchased for them. What a project! The whole family got involved. Needless to say each child got an (A) once it was turned into the teacher that next fall. Their work was on display for the whole year, only to return home when that year class was over.

John and Rebecca felt their children were growing up entirely too fast. Everett was to graduate high school soon. Gwen had left right after she graduated college to work at the very same hospital her mother and Beatrice had worked at long ago. Beatrice had still worked there until just a few years ago and was able to help Gwen get a nursing position. Gwen had been working there now since June of 1931. Their oldest daughter, Elizabeth was now planning a small church wedding in March of 1932. So yes the family was growing up very fast and leaving home one by one. Rebecca would cry every time she would think of these things.

Dale Henderson and James George had become very close of late. Although Dale was three years older than James, no one would ever know this. James was bigger than Dale. They called each other Dutch and Duke and pretended to be riding the western ranges. They imagined these things when told to go get the milking cattle of an evening. This made the project fun instead of work. When they were smaller they would take a stick that Rebecca had sewn horse heads upon and ride off into the blue wonder. Now they would hop onto the back of their old mare bare backed and they would ride together out over the pasture. Many evenings Rebecca would watch them until they were completely out of her site, praying neither would get bounced off of that old horse.

# C hapter 9

John, being born August the 12<sup>th</sup> of 1881, had just turned fifty years old in the year of 1931. Late in that year, Rebecca noticed he would come into the house and sometimes go straight to the bedroom and lie down. The reading time he had devoted each night to the older children when they were small was now reduced for the younger children to only a few minutes a couple of nights a week. James George had prided himself to being a pretend preacher. He would get one of John's ties and get upon a small stool and preach until he could preach no more. John had always thought this was very cute and wonderful. He called him his little preacher man. He would tell the child to come to him so he could straighten up his tie and then he would take a comb from his pocket and make sure the lad's hair was combed properly. He would tell him a minister must always look his very best. Rebecca loved to watch the interaction with James George and his father. She would often smile the whole time this was going on.

This one particular night, John had whispered to Rebecca that he thought James was overly loud tonight. He told of how he wished he had a way to get him to stop without discouraging his little minister ways. Just as Rebecca started to walk away to put a stop to the noise made by James George; John caught her by her dress hem. He chuckled and said,

"I would prefer to silence the little preacher without upsetting God."

With that remark, Rebecca let out a giggle. Even though she was still smiling, she knew something was wrong and knew it was very important to quiet the place down. The littlest girls were playing with paper dolls in the floor. Mabel was sitting in a corner chair reading what must have been a very interesting book; because Dale Henderson was sitting nearby listening, seemly spellbound by every word. Rebecca talked them all into going upstairs to play. She ask James George if he would like to go upstairs and preach to his sisters. This worked very well and all five little angels followed one after another to the top of the stairs.

Rebecca followed John to the bedroom as he sat down on the bed and put his head in his hands while saying,

"Becky, I did not want to alarm you but I have been having some really terrible headaches lately."

Rebecca sat down beside of John and wrapped her arms around his shoulders while asking,

"What do you think is wrong?"

He said he had no idea unless it was some sort of flu or something. He went on to say, he had no other signs of the flu. Naturally Rebecca became very concerned, but did not want John to know just how worried she had become. She had been noticing him looking really hollow-eyed lately.

She also noticed redness in his eyes that just seemed to linger for days. This night she went to the kitchen and fixed a mustard poultice. This was done by stuffing cheese cloth with heated mustard seeds and stems along with mush and other herbs. She then wrapped it up as if it were a scarf and took it into the bedroom and laid it upon John's head. She heard him say Ah-h-h as she left the room. Maybe this would help him with the pain.

As the weeks went by, the practice of making a mustard poultice became a common place happening. Every evening John needed one and his pain seemed to grow with each passing day. Rebecca had insisted he go see Doc Brown in Vinton and he finally did. The doctor told him it could be stress or maybe he was over working at his age. From that day on, John tried harder to hide his pain, but Rebecca knew he was suffering. She just did not know what to do about it.

Rebecca had purchased some salve ointment from the traveling store that stopped by the farm ever so often. This was a closed in truck that had back doors that opened up. It had about everything anyone would need. John and Rebecca would often buy sugars, salts and some penny candy for the children when this truck came by. They knew old Mr. Swick who operated this business, and Rebecca had told him of John's headaches on his last trip. So he had done some research and found this ointment. It was red in color and had a very strong smell. Someone had told Mr. Swick it was really a good cure for about any kind of pain. So, faithfully every evening after the purchase Rebecca would attend to the cures that they had available. But John was not getting any better. He was only getting worse.

Spring finally came in the year of 1931 and the weather seemed to cause John to feel a lot better. He was able to tend to his chores. He and the older children planted the fields and he started believing and convincing Rebecca he had just had some sort of virus during the winter. He still had the headaches, but they did seem to be further apart. Rebecca still worried that maybe he had just learned to live with the pain and now he knew how to hide it better. Although his pains were farther apart, he did admit that when he did have one they were sharper and much more painful than those before. He was very careful to always wear a hat when in the sun and Rebecca kept a close eye on him to make sure he stopped working long enough to take a drink of water every so often.

There was this neighbor boy who attended their church and lived on the farm that adjoined theirs in the back. He seemed to be hanging out more and more at the Dahl farm. Rebecca knew it was because he was sweet on Mabel. She just did not know how long it was going to take John to figure that one out. This young man's grandfather had also acquired land for payment of his services as a Colonel to the United States Army, just the same as John's grandfather. These families had connections for years. The boy's family was from the same part of Virginia as the Dahl family. After attending the same church now for many years Rebecca had become close to the boy's mother.

Each spring, like all of the farm people around there, Rebecca and her family would take all the furniture from within the house and place it outside. This was called spring cleaning and very necessary because of the heating systems one used. Rugs were beaten to remove the dirt. Beds
110

and pillows would be emptied and the covers washed or replaced, then filled again with either feathers or straw. Walls were brushed down and a sort of clay would be used to clean the wall papers. Kitchens and any kind of cupboards would be painted, usually with the same paint as the walls. The outside of the house would be whitewashed or sometimes painted depending on whether one could afford the paint. In John and Rebecca's case, they chose to paint the front of the house about every five to ten years and would white wash the back of the house every year. Left over whitewash would then be used to paint part way up from the roots of the trees. This kept bugs and worms off the fruit trees and just looked pretty on the other trees.

Everyone seemed to have pretty lace curtains. This was the style of the day. These curtains would be washed and starched. Being of a fine crochet they then had to be stretched. The mother of this young man who had taken such an interest in Mabel seemed to be the only person in the community who owned a pair of curtain stretchers. Each household had to plan their cleaning around the usage of these stretchers. Rebecca always had borrowed the curtain stretchers from Mrs. Wyman. Mr. Wyman also had helped many times at the Dahl farm. The whole community came together in harvest time. When hay needed put up, men would come from all over the hills to help each other. John and the boys would go to their farms to help them as well. The boy's father, Mr. Wyman had the only thrashing machine in the area. He would bring it over to the Dahl farm to make hay stacks. Putting up hay was always a nice time for all the neighbors. It was very hard work. Once it was done, which was usually late evening, the workers would go to the house of whoever's farm they were working on. That housewife would have prepared a wonderful hot meal for the group. If anyone played an instrument, they would play and sing until time to leave. Everyone seemed to really enjoy these times.

Mrs. Wyman also got deep into all of the holiday celebrations. She was such a sweet, bubbly woman. One could not help but be happy around her. She radiated happiness! Christmas, she would organize a play with the young people at the church and this was always extraordinary. Halloween was really big for her as well. She would make costumes for all of her children and one for herself. She was always the person who took the neighboring children door to door over the country side to trick or treat. She entertained the youth at church the whole year 'round and taught their Sunday school class. She would organize all of the church events. Mrs. Wyman would have ice cream socials, hay rides and camp fires. All the young people loved her so very much.

Rebecca could not be too concerned with Byron Wyman wanting to be around her daughter. She and John both thought a lot of this young man and of his family. Rebecca felt sure if these two young people became an item she would not oppose. By the spring of 1931 Byron Wyman was a constant helper around the Dahl farm. He would hurry with his chores at home so he could walk across the field and help Mr. Dahl. This was a relief to Rebecca because she knew John did not feel well at all anymore and he could use all the
112

help he could get. This gave him several young men working on the chores to where he could just more or less supervise. Of course she did not get much help out of Mabel inside the house anymore. She would get through with her chores with lightning speed and then she was off volunteering to ride in the wagon to pick up corn, wheat or whatever the crop may be.

One afternoon as Rebecca went to take water and sandwiches to the field, she noticed Byron and Mabel taking a break. They were sitting upon a fence giggling. When she arrived at the team and wagon she remarked to John that those two seemed to be pretty cozy. John laughed and said,

"Oh, you're just now noticing that."
So, he knew all along and obviously felt the same as Rebecca and he seemed to have no objections.

Fall harvest came and went. Bryon was also spending many evenings around their place now. By this time he had asked John's permission to court Mabel. John had given him his approval. The couple spent many evenings in the parlor listening to the Victrola. They would sing and giggle until someone would say it was time for Bryon to leave. He was such a nice young man! He usually had watched the clock on the wall himself and was always well aware the curfew time had arrived. Rebecca thought of how much more quiet he seemed to be than that of her children. He was so polite, but rarely spoke unless you started talking with him first.

Everett had a girlfriend too and John would let him use the Model T during better weather to visit her. His girlfriend lived a good fifteen or twenty miles away and Rebecca would always
113

worry until he returned. Gwen almost never got to come home, but she was sharing an efficiency apartment with Alice, Bea's daughter. The two girls lived together just as their mothers had done years before. Rebecca knew they were having great fun and knew they would become very close, just as she and Beatrice had done. She knew they were telling each other everything and sharing in their dreams. She couldn't help but wish Bea lived closer so they too could discuss everything as they once did. There were so many times she needed her sister. With John showing signs of some illness it would be nice to confer with another nurse who might have some sort of a solution.

Gwen was not going to get to come home for Christmas this year. One comfort for Rebecca however, was that she knew she would still be with family members. Gwen would be spending the holidays with Robert and Beatrice. Unlike having a small tree in a corner of an apartment as she and Bea used to have. Oh she was sure Alice and Gwen had some sort of a tree anyway within that tiny apartment. Both girls were very tight mouthed about whether either of them had a beau or not. This kept the mothers guessing and asking an awful lot of questions. Gwen would sometimes answer her mother's letters by just sending a poem. She would as if ignore the questioning of her mother. She was so poetic anyway. She would write things like:

"My mother should know that when I had to go, my life would be different from the farm life. She should quit asking questions and just be nice and try to take everything in strife."
She would always sign,
114

"BUT, I LOVE YOU MOTHER, Daddy too, and while you're thinking about that, tell the bigger ones and the little rascals I love them also."

Everett might as well be away from home, judging by the time he spent with his girlfriend Hazel. Their daughter Elizabeth had put in an application at a school in Rutland, Ohio. As everyone had expected, she did get the position. She would be working as a teacher of the first grade at that school. This school was probably about thirty miles away from the Dahl farm. She and her husband-to-be had put a down payment on a farm very close to that area. At least the couple had purchased something a few miles closer to their parents. Their new farm was just this side of a small town named Danville.

While at the school for the interview, Elizabeth had spoken with the master of the school about her brother dating a girl from that area. She told him the girl's name was Hazel Nash. The master had spoken very highly of that family. He said the Nash family was very active in the main church of Danville, Ohio. This made Elizabeth happy knowing she would probably be attending that same church after her marriage and their move. Upon hearing this news, it caused a big relief to John and Rebecca. They had always hoped each child would find a nice church going partner. Now, if they only had the chance to meet this young lady named Hazel. Everett was still very young; therefore they weren't sure the couple's relationship would last. They did however, have a lot of faith in their children and their choices. So far so good! Each choice the older children had made to this point was good ones.

115

# C hapter 10

Christmas came and went. John had been in bed most of the holidays. John, Jr., Everett and the boys had kept the fire wood cut and all the children had taken care of the chores. Sunday morning's John was always ready to go to church. But, during the month of December he would often try to get up to go, however his headaches would become more severe. He would have to lie back down. Rebecca had asked Everett to stop at Dr. Browns while on a visit to see Hazel. She wanted him to ask the doctor if he could come to the house one day, of course at his convenience, to check on John again. She knew John would never approve of this. NO way, NO how! He would believe the cost would be more than they could afford.

The week of James George's birthday, which was the 27$^{th}$ of December 1932, he was to be ten years old. This being a very special double digit year, Rebecca decided to have friends over and to cook a special meal with cake and candles. Everett brought Hazel for the very first time. He had just told the family the week before he had gotten brave enough on Christmas day to ask her father for permission to marry her. The father had said yes, but only if they waited a good ways out in the future. They agreed to the terms and of course she had accepted his proposal.

Hazel was beautiful and everyone loved her immediately. James was the first to say anything upon her arrival. He ran to the door when he heard the car pull up. He waited patiently until Hazel stepped inside the door. This little guy never met a stranger. He was the friendliest little fellow. He looked up at Hazel with those great big pretty blue eyes and threw his arms around her legs and gave her a big hug. He then said, as if one of the older children had put him up to it,

"Even though you have not married our brother yet, we would like to welcome you into our family."

It sounded very much rehearsed. Rebecca knew the older children were proud of his representation because everyone was smiling when he gave his little speech. Then he added something Rebecca knew was of his own making,

"Gee, you sure are pretty and I'm glad you came to my birthday party!"

John had managed to sit up. Rebecca had moved his favorite chair into the parlor just the week before. The parlor was only used when the family had company or when one of the older children was using it for courting. They usually didn't even heat that room during the winter. Since this was the front door and if one knew someone was coming, they would start a fire in that room only at that time to entertain guest.

This was a very pretty room. The long tall windows touched the floor. Rebecca had decorated these long windows with nice lace

118

curtains. The rods that held the curtains were of a dark mahogany with large spinals on each end. The way the curtains were made at the top, it looked as if someone had crocheted four or five rows to go around the rod, then waited another four or five rows and covered the rod again. The front door looked like it was made in square panels. The glass in the upper part of the door was smoked with a flower like design. The rustic door knob had a skeleton key hanging from it. Rebecca always thought it looked like a dirty rust, but the darken door knob with its floral design just added to the charm.

If one stood in the middle of this room and looked at each item as they twirled around they would see a large clock hanging on the wall immediately beside the door hinges and right before you reached the first large window. This clock had been in Rebecca's family forever and she counted herself very lucky to be the one who got it. It had a glass door over the chime. The chime was not made as everyone else's would be with the round medallion. This clock had a boy and a girl in a swing and as the clock went tick-tock, the little boy and girl would swing. It was a big fascination to all children. Adults remarked much about it as well!

Between the two floor length windows on two walls in this room was the couch that sat at an angle. This caused a large corner space behind it. The couch was of mohair in a dark maroon color, or maybe it was closer to a wine color. In the next corner was the tall backed mahogany piano with its claw feet and a bench. There was a lace dolly on the top of the piano where Rebecca had tastefully arranged family pictures. Next was the

119

door to the seating room that led to the kitchen and other rooms. All doors were tall and in missionary styling. The casings were wide and each had about a ten by ten inch square at the corners. These squares had a swirl design carved into them. Across from the piano was the entrance to the stairway with a stairway door made the same as the others. Then just to the left of that door was a potbellied stove during the winter months. On that same wall was the Victrola. In the summer months this potbellied stove and the one in the family room would be removed from the house. Pretty flower painted covers were designed so that they would pop right into the chimney holes. Summer months the Victrola would be moved to the middle of that parlor wall and placed where the stove once was.

In this room was a large oval picture. The frame was of a wide beautiful gold wood carved designed frame. It got moved around a lot, but most of the time it was right above the Victrola. This picture was of John and Rebecca. The picture was of their wedding day. It only showed the top of each of them; just their heads and shoulders. The photographer had done such a beautiful job. Rebecca's hair was standing high in a bun. Beatrice had curled smaller sections of her hair and had it falling down around her cheeks. This formed sort of a halo look around that beautiful face. The pretty dress she had worn looked regal in this picture and the cameo stood out in the middle of that high lace collar. John's hair looked darker in the picture because he had it slicked back. He had on a tall stiff collar and a dark suit. Every time Rebecca passed this picture she would think of how John just had to be the

120

best looking man on earth. She would always believe that to be true. Somehow the photographer had shaped the actual photo like an egg while letting it fade out into a plain shadowed area before it reached the frame. Rebecca loved this picture.

The floor that had been non-existent upon their arrival to this farm; now was of a wide planked mahogany colored wood. The flooring was pretty by itself, but John and Rebecca had covered most of it with a large mohair wine colored rug for warmth. They had put this rug into the room somewhat irregular. They placed it from one corner to another while leaving large triangles at each corner. This showed off the pretty wood floors.

Now the view would be about back to the front door, however someone could take a right turn before reaching that front door. This would take you past the long closet under the stairway. If you kept going you would go right into John and Rebecca's bedroom. On the wall beside the closet under the stairs and before the closet door was a painting of some deer in a forest. John's family had given them this painting. It was so remarkable because it had been painted by a blind woman, as crazy as that may sound. It was truly painted by a blind woman. It was so beautiful! It had grey backgrounds as if it were night or evening in that forest. Rebecca would look at it sometimes for several minutes trying to imagine how a blind woman could have painted from her heart, something so very beautiful! Surely she must have been able to see at one time. No one had told the whole story of the painting. This whole room was just very special to Rebecca. Even she found it very hard to believe this is the very same room that had a tree growing through it upon her arrival many years ago.

With John's health getting worse they had moved his favorite chair to the spot where the Victrola usually sat. They had placed the Victrola behind the couch now in the corner. Due to John's health, the family had also started building a fire daily in that room. It held heat better than the adjoining rooms because you could shut all of the doors. The family had placed John's chair close to the heat. This also gave him more quiet time when he was able to sit up. Tonight he was sitting in that chair by the stove. The oil lights were lit and he looked very pale as the light danced all around him. He had some claims of freezing earlier and Rebecca had thrown a quilt over his lap, thus making him look even frailer in the light.

John tried so hard to be normal to the guest. He chuckled when Hazel walked into the room. He agreed with James by saying,

"I couldn't have said it better myself young man."

Then John repeated James George's statement by saying,

"Gee Hazel, you sure are pretty!"

He reached up for a hug. Rebecca could not help but notice he could hardly left himself from the chair. He then said,

"We would be most honored to have you as an addition to our happy family, but as your father told you, Everett's mother and I agree that you must wait until you are older."

John must have wanted to get that sentence out of the way right up front. Rebecca knew John was in pain, but the evening went by with him sitting up

122

for the entire time. She knew he had forced himself to stay up. She also felt he would probably pay for that later.

As soon as Everett left to take Hazel home, Rebecca went straight to the kitchen to fix a mustard poultice. What were they going to do about those headaches? They seem to be getting closer together. One could tell by looking at John's face they were getting more painful. He had lost more weight. He was also getting so he could hardly eat a thing.

That evening, as every evening anymore, Rebecca would see that the children were tucked away into their beds then go to tend to John. She would hold him for hours, rubbing his head and telling him how much she loved him. She would often ask him how he or she would have survived without each other. He would always say,

"I would not have wanted to live without you Darling. You can never know how much I love you."
Tonight he said,

"I knew you were meant for me the very day you caught your petticoat on that nail. You looked so beautiful; all the while your pretty cheeks were turning a rose pink. It nearly embarrassed you to death, but I had never seen one so beautiful. I could not help but just stare. I knew from that very moment, I had to make you mine somehow. You were the beautiful woman of my dreams."
She then asked him,

"Have you ever changed your mind dear?"
He snapped right back with a,

"Yes."

This took her by surprise and she pretended to slap him. He laughed and said,

"Yes, I have changed my mind. I ended up loving you more than I ever thought possible and you were more beautiful than those dreams. I know you love me too Becky. Have I ever said thank you for being so beautiful, so wonderful, so-o-o sweet and such a kind wonderful mother?"
John hesitated for a minute then said,

"I know you're worried darling, but don't be afraid. If I should die before my time our life will not end here, we will always be together."
He then said,

"I am afraid as well Becky, I don't want to leave you to fend for yourself and put all these burdens upon you. I am supposed to protect you and provide for you and our children. I pray every day that God will lift this burden from us, at least until the children are grown. But I also know that God has a plan on everything. Therefore, I end my prayers by saying 'Have thine own way Lord'. If it is God's will to take me, we will be together again in Heaven someday. You know that Darling."

Rebecca was so glad the lights were off. John seemed to be verifying the bad feelings she had been getting of late. She had feelings of how he may not make it or live very much longer. This is the reason she had ask for Dr. Brown unbeknownst to her husband. She started to cry but knew she had to be strong for John and just prayed a silent prayer for God to give her strength. What would she do without her beloved husband? She too, had prayed every day that those headaches would go away and his health would be restored. She did not know about the *Have Thine*
124

***Own Way Lord*** <u>Part</u> of John's wishes. Guessing she was maybe too selfish to add that to her prayers. Oh, to have the belief and the strength of John. Tonight had just justified her fears. John believed he was going to die.

Doctor Brown showed up at about two o'clock on the next Monday. He seemed very concerned even before he walked into the door. Everett must have told him his father was getting worse every day. The kind old gentleman, with his thick glasses, stood a head above Rebecca. As he looked at her in the eyes, he seemed to be looking over those glasses into her very soul. He was looking at her with a really worried look. He had a watch chain hanging from his neat dark suit and she had noticed every time she saw him he was messing with that chain. He often pulled out his watch to look at the time. Today, he did not do that. Instead, he took both of her hands into his and said,

"How are you doing my dear?"
She said,
"Fine."
She knew by his all-knowing eyes that he knew the truth. He told her she looked tired and was way too pale. He asked her not to let herself get worn down. He stated that she needed to stay strong for everyone. She knew all of this to be true and wished he would not concern himself with her and just go on in and heal John.

The doctor examined John for a long time. He listened to his heart. Checked his whole body over and then took his temperature. The whole time John was asking what he was doing there, saying he felt fine and complaining behind the doctor's back. Every time the doctor's back was turned, John kept moving his lips and mouthing to Rebecca,

"Did you call for him?"

She shot him a strong look and mouthed back at him,

"Yes, I did. I was worried!"

The doctor finally finished with his examination and just sat and talked with John awhile. He asked him how his crops did this year and of how the new insecticides were working out on his orchard. Dr. Brown told John he had heard some of his children were getting married off and asked if that made him feel any older. They sat and talked for a good hour. Rebecca could not believe the good doctor did not have to be somewhere else. She kept wondering about the nervous habit he had of looking at his watch. What was going on with him today?

Finally Doctor Brown got up to leave. He shook John's hand while holding it in his for an extra-long time. He told him what a good patient and friend he had always been. He asked him not to be too upset with Rebecca over asking him to come out today. He stated in a firm voice that Rebecca had a right to be worried. He told him how he hoped the liquid medicine he had brought would relieve some of the pain. He said to be sure to tell Rebecca of the headaches as he felt one coming on. It was easier to prevent some of the pain if given the medicine immediately. Rebecca was instructed while in that room to give John the medicine when asked. This should cause the pain to be less severe.

The good doctor then walked out of the room while motioning for Rebecca to follow him. As they walked out into the parlor the doctor told
126

her to give him the red liquid four times a day and the white color liquid anytime as he needed it, He then told her if she ran out of either, she was to send one of the children after some more immediately! She took him through the kitchen so they could speak without John hearing them. Rebecca ask,

"What on earth is wrong with him doctor?" First the doctor didn't speak. He just shook his head over and over again. Then he answered by saying,

"I just don't know Rebecca. I have ruled out everything I can think of, but I can tell you this; at this rate with him losing so much weight he will not last long if things don't change."

A shocked look came over Rebecca's face as she realized at that minute why the doctor had spent so much time with her beloved husband. The doctor realized Rebecca knew at that point as well. He hugged her tightly in his arms and just let her cry. He had been a friend of the Dahl's for many years and she feared the worst. She knew he had spent a big part of his day to take the time to say goodbye to a dear old friend.

After the doctor left, Rebecca put on that brave smile and went back into the bedroom. She leaned over and kissed her loving husband on the forehead. Then she kissed him on the cheek and she told him she loved him. She then mustered up her calmest voice and told him that this medicine would surely help. She even found a voice in her that added,

"Maybe you will get well now darling." When she heard those words coming out of her mouth ever so smoothly; she started to shake. She knew now deep in her heart this was not the case.

This was not the case at all! She held John for as long as she could without breaking down. She asked him if he was feeling better now and he told her the medicine had helped but it was making him drossy. She told him she must go take care of some chores. Then she left the room.

As Rebecca left their bedroom, she could feel hot tears flowing down her face. She darted through the house and out the back door. She wasn't sure her legs would carry her past the coal shed. It was about five-hundred yards from the house. She was trying to reach the next shed that held her old white buggy. She made it there and then climbed up into that buggy. Here she knew she would be hid from everyone. Once she got into the seat, she bawled her eyes out. She did not even try to wipe the tears away, she just let them flow. Oh, how she needed to just let go of those tears. Finally she got down on her knees and prayed to God. She knew the way her husband was suffering she could not expect him to want to hold on much longer. She started to feel selfish with her need to hang onto him. How cruel could she be. God and the doctor needed to heal him. She did not want to hang onto John just for him to suffer?

Rebecca started her prayers by telling God that John was a young man. She asked why this burden had come upon him.

"Why us Lord?"

She kept asking God. She knew she had to regain her composure before she could go back into the house. She had heard Mabel holler for her a little earlier. She climbed slowly down from the buggy and walked towards the barn where she tried to walk off the stress. She hoped her eyes would clear up some before returning to the house. She started walking back toward the house just as Mabel was coming to look for her. She knew now trying to hide the eyes was not going to work. Her daughter asked immediately,

"Mother, what is wrong?"
All the children had been asking questions as to what was wrong with their father lately as it was. Rebecca knew Mabel was old enough to know, so they sat down on some barrels by the garage and had a big talk. Rebecca told Mabel to prepare herself because her father more than likely would not be with them much longer. She told her the only way John was going to survive was if God took hold of the situation. She told Mabel of how the doctor had told her this very thing just today in not so many words. Mabel looked at her mother with a shocked look and started to cry. Rebecca hugged her very tight and begged her to please keep strong and told her of how she needed to keep her face strong in front of the other children.

Rebecca told Mabel she and her father were going to have to depend on their older children even more in these days to come. She told her of how she had so much faith in each one of her beautiful children and of how much she loved them. She said she was so very proud of them. She also asked Mabel to draft a letter to Gwen and to ask her to come home to see her father. She wanted Mabel to ask Gwen to take off some extra time from work. She said to tell Gwen they would help with the expenses of the trip. Rebecca told Mabel to stress that it was of utmost importance that she come home. Mabel and Rebecca gathered themselves together and headed back for the house.
129

In the days that followed, Rebecca had the same long talks with each of the older children. After informing each one of them of the dire circumstances, she would get down on her knees with them and they would pray for their father's health. Rebecca's hope was that this would ease their pain and maybe God would listen to their pleas.

Mabel had told Bryon of the problem and Mrs. Wyman had been over several times to visit. She had also requested prayer for Mr. Dahl at their church. Many neighbors stopped by in the days and weeks that followed. The whole countryside was praying for them and Rebecca prayed that the Good Lord would hear their prayers and spare John. She knew if it was God's will, he would surely be spared because of all of these wonderful God fearing Christians who were praying so hard for his recovery.

January seemed to be extra cold this year and some of the neighbors came by to help cut wood for the fires. Ethel, John's sister had been told of her brothers depleting health and had called in the rest of his brothers and sisters to visit. John would tell everyone of how they should not have come and taken the time out of their busy schedules. Ethel would always try to reassure him and the others that John had some sort of virus that would just go away soon. Rebecca believed she was trying to convince herself as much as she was trying to convince the others.

Ethel would come to visit and stay with John for hours on end. She would only leave when she knew she had to prepare a meal for her own family. She would tell him how she had always looked up to her big brother and of how
130

proud she was of him. She would often read to him and place wet towels upon his head. Rebecca could feel Ethel's pain and knew that Ethel really felt in her heart her brother would not be around for very much longer. All anyone could do was hope something would change.

The severity of John's headaches worsened with each passing day. He and Rebecca tried everything in their power to stop the pain that he was enduring. The only thing that seemed to help was the mustard poultice. These poultices smelled so badly that the smell would hit you the minute you walked into the house. The smaller children complained about the smell, but they understood when mother told them it made father feel better. The younger children had been asking a lot of questions about daddy lately. They wondered why their father slept so much.

John's illness was very hard on their youngest child Bella who was only five years old. John used to sit in his chair and rock her until she went to sleep just about every evening. He would read her a fairy tale or small little stories from the Bible. Bella just could not understand why daddy had stopped doing that. He would now often request she be brought to him in his room where he would let her lay down beside of him. He would just hug her for a while. She would come out somewhat bewildered looking and asking why her daddy was sick. It was not any easier for Edith nor for James George. It was just plain hard to explain these sorts of things to the younger children. One could see too much suffering in the eyes of the older children at the thought of losing their father. How would the little ones understand it at all? How could a mother put this kind of pain on a younger child?  Maybe it was best to try to put a happy face on for each of them and just try to go on.

Rebecca noticed all the children were extra quiet anymore.  She had not heard James George preach one time in weeks.  Edith and Bella seemed to be off in some corner somewhere most of the time.  You could hear a pin drop around them.  It was also very noticeable that the groups that usually hung out together were now often caught just sitting alone somewhere while just staring out into space.  Watching the pain each child was bearing was killing Rebecca.  Oh the pain this was causing the entire family.  She also could hear the girls crying a lot at night.  She prayed John could not hear them.  The whole matter just broke Rebecca's heart.

# C hapter 11

Tragedy struck the Dahl family on January 24th, 1932.    Just one month after Christmas.   John Dahl died at the age of fifty, leaving a family of nine children and a wife who adored him.    The nurse daughter Gwen had requested one month off from work after her sister Mabel had ask her to come home.   With the traveling arrangements and the need to be home to help her family, the hospital understood and told her the time off would not jeopardize her position. She had arrived just two days before John's passing.   She and the rest of the family felt so blessed for her to have been able to have been there to see her father before he went away.

The three days of mourning passed with Rebecca hardly knowing what was going on around her.  She remembered many people coming to her home.  She realized her sisters and brothers were there, but could not remember when they arrived.   She knew John's brothers and sisters were there as well.   She did remember Beatrice and Robert came in the day before the funeral. She wasn't sure how any of those who traveled by train had gotten from the train stations to her

133

house. Maybe the older children had gone to pick them up. She just did not know. She was just walking around in a haze.

The funeral home had placed wreaths upon the doors and placed signs along the roads. This was to tell drivers to please drive slow out of respect of course, but also for safety. Each sign stated that there had been a death in the family. The signs were of a triangle and had the words "Death in the Family."

During this period, people who passed away were taken to a mortuary. They were taken care of, bathed and dressed in their very best of clothing and then the body was returned to a relative's home until the day of the burial. Rebecca remembers her brother-in-law Andy telling her not to worry about a thing. He said he would see that everything was taken care of. She had handed her brother-in-law John's only suit. Elizabeth had ironed a crisp white shirt for her father to wear. Her brother-in-law took care of the rest. She was coherent enough to know that everyone had stayed up all night for a wake one of those nights and she knew there seemed to be food all over the place. She did not know from where the food cometh.

On the morning before the funeral Beatrice took Rebecca by the hand and took her upstairs. She told her she had to pick out a dress to wear. Beatrice informed her sister that she had already been through her closet down stairs and had not found a black dress. She had now taken her search upstairs where she had laid out a black suit-dress. She had remembered this dress from their younger days and had found it in one of the old trunks. She had shaken it out and had pressed it. Her opinion was that the dress still looked very nice. She had
134

also picked out a hat in black that had a veil coming down over the face. Rebecca imagined if she had been herself, she would have argued with Beatrice about that dress. She would have believed it was too small, too fancy or something. Not being herself, she put it on. It was as if she was out of her body and someone else was carrying on for her. Surprisingly, after twenty some odd years the dress did still fit.

On the day of the funeral, Rebecca could remember John, Jr. checking out all the children to see if they were dressed properly. The older girls checked to see if the smaller children's little faces were clean. They then lined each of them up like little toy soldiers. Rebecca would always remember that walk to the Model T. Each pale and sad little child was walking in unison to be seated in whichever car someone wanted each to ride in. Chancy took two of the boys along with Robert and Beatrice. Their children were getting into cars further back in the line. There seemed to be several automobiles and people just seemed to keep getting into them. It was as if they all had rehearsed for a movie or something. No one said a word.

The two miles to the church were the shortest two miles Rebecca had ever traveled. She hoped everything would go in slow motion as she knew she would soon have to say goodbye to the very biggest part of her soul. She kept telling herself to be strong, but that little message she was telling herself just did not work anymore. She wondered how she was even breathing. All she could do was whisper,

"Oh God, *Why*? *Why*? *Why*? Why John?" This kind of questioning was completely against

135

all of their religious beliefs. She knew she was not to question God, but she just could not stop.

Upon arrival, one of Rebecca's brothers led her into the church and one of her son's was on the other side of her. She was not even aware of which brother or which son. All she knew at this minute was that she just wanted to die herself. The church was full of people. It looked as if some were even standing. This was a small church and she thought that they must be standing due to the lack of seats. The organ was playing. There were flowers everywhere. She wondered where the flowers could have come from in such cold weather. It looked as if it was going to snow. She was praying it would just go ahead and do that. Maybe that way no one could put her beloved John into the ground.

Once everyone was seated the service began. Rebecca heard the minister say,

"God givith and God takith away."

Then different people got up and each was telling of how great a person John was. Then just as fast as it began, a prayer was said and it was all over. People began flowing up one by one to pay their respects to her beloved Mr. John H. Dahl. Rebecca sat there just hurting and staring at the casket with tears flowing non-stop at this point. She thought everyone had done a very good job of telling of the greatness of John. But, she felt only if they really knew how wonderful this man was to his wife and his children. She wanted to scream that there in that casket is the most wonderful man that will ever walk the face of this earth. She watched as each person in the church walked by his casket. Many friends and family members

136

were in tears. Everyone stopped and offered their condolences to Rebecca and the children.

Finally it came time for each of Rebecca's little family to go up to say goodbye to their Father and her Husband for the very last time. The children all looked ash white and some had cried until they could not cry anymore. Rebecca hugged each and every one of them as they stood by the casket. She told them of how sorry she was that they had lost their father. She tried to comfort her children as she knew the loss of John was not just her loss. She knew her children were suffering just as much.

The time came for Rebecca to stand before John by herself for the very last time. While tears flowed down her cheeks, she leaned over to kiss her husband goodbye. He was so cold. Oh how she wanted to just crawl in there with him. How could she go on without John? She stood there for as long as anyone would allow. Finally John Jr. walked up and said,

"Mother we need to go."

He and Dale took her by the arms and started leading her down the aisle and then out of the church. She could feel her legs weakening. It was as if they were going from beneath her. The men just got a stronger grip on her and lead her straight to the awaiting car. She kept looking back and begging them to let her stay with John. Knowing she was not making any sense, she calmed down when Dale said not to worry they were bringing John along with them.

Once again, everyone loaded into the cars. This time she seemed more aware of what was in front of her and she focused her eyes on that hearse, seeing it through all of her tears. As the

137

hearse moved along in front of her car; the site burned into her brain to where she knew she would remember it always. She just stared at it while traveling the two or so miles to the cemetery.

It was a very good thing it had not snowed in over a week now. It was also good there was not much dampness on the roads. The roads to the cemetery would have been impassable. At another forks in the road just about a mile above their house was a small road that took off through the country. Guesses are that one could say it was more of a path than a road. It stayed in even worse shape than the main roads. Once it split again so far out, you started up a hill. The road was barely wide enough for a car and it was dug through the hillside. Both sides of the road reached far above the cars to where all one could see when they looked out of a car window were large dirt walls. The ruts or ditches on each side of the grassy spot in the middle of the road were so deep the cars dragged on the bottom when driving over them. Different people had voiced their concern about how that long procession was going to make it up that hill.

Once again the trip was way too short for Rebecca. As the procession got to the family cemetery Rebecca had the odd thought of how thankful she was that John had sent the boys over to mow later than usual last fall. What a dumb thought. Who cared if people saw old dead grass, she had just lost her husband. As the hearse pulled through the black iron gates, she started crying more valiantly. She could not suppress the sounds any longer. The children who were in that car with her were crying as well. No one could get out of the car on cue. Finally they composed themselves to be able to march down the narrow path to the grave site.

The minister spoke for a few minutes and prayed dust to dust and so on. Everyone who wanted a flower took one and Rebecca just sat there staring while feeling as if her life was over. While praying at the grave site, the minister had said in his prayer,

"Lord, give this family the strength to handle the loss of one so dear."

Thoughts and questions kept racing through Rebecca's mind as to why God had chosen to take so many loved ones from her. So many of her family had been taken way before their time. She had felt when she lost her mother and her father that they were not old enough to die. Now she had lost a young husband. She kept talking to God as if He could bring John back. As if He just understood that He needed to bring him back by saying things like,

"You took a man who had little children. He has a ten year old, a seven year old and a five year old."

Dale Henderson was only three years older than that. Mabel a couple years older and the others were just trying to get started out in their adult life. Each and every one of them needed their father. How could they all deal with this? The whole time she was wondering how she could be of any good to any of them if she could not stop falling apart herself.

Rebecca could see the feelings everyone around her was having. She knew everyone was feeling so sorry for this young woman with nine children who was now left alone with no means of support other than what could be dug out of the ground of their farm. Everyone believed the older children would be okay, but were very concerned about the younger children. She was going to have to show some strength to keep both sides of the family from believing that raising the children would be entirely too much for her. She realized she was a small dainty little woman and there were many physical things she may not be able to manage, but she also knew there was going to be no choice in what she had to do.

Leaving that cemetery she knew she must shake herself out of the hopelessness and show everyone she was stronger than they gave her credit. From that day on Rebecca cried in silence, she went off to be by herself when she could not stop the tears. She got a renewed strength inside of her that was unmatched by most mortals. She took charge of her life and became the rock of her family.

# C hapter 12

Elizabeth was going to get married soon and start teaching school on a full time basis. Gwen was working as a registered nurse now. This made her mother very proud. John, Jr., who was now twenty-two, would keep the farm going along with the help of his brothers. John, Jr. had long ago made the choice to be a farmer. He made that choice while still in school. He seemed very devoted and loved farming just as his father had always loved it. His intentions were to keep the farm running just as if his father were still there. In reality, he had been doing just that for many months now anyway following the fading of his father's health.

Everett and Hazel would be getting married in a year or so. This had worried Rebecca because she knew she would be losing one hand at the farm. However, just a few days ago, Everett had told his mother he would like to fix up the old long cabin. This old cabin was on the bottom section of the latest purchased part of the farm. Everett felt this would keep him and his future on the farm. Thus providing him to help his brother keep the business of their farm profitable and continue working in the same way as usual.

141

Rebecca thought she must have agreed to Everett's idea about the cabin in one of their conversations, but nothing seemed sure in her mind right now. She seemed to be operating in some kind of a daze. Everything said or done just seemed to her to be in slow motion. Things someone would say would hit her only after much delay. So a day or two after Everett's proposal, it hit her. All of a sudden she thought that re-working that old cabin was probably a very good idea. Yet she realized the old cabin was in a very bad shape. She remembered John had some lumber behind the wheat bins and suggested to Everett that he could use it. She also believed there were some sheets of glass behind the chicken house. So maybe with a little energy; Everett would be able to make a home out of that cabin.

Rebecca could not remember one day from another for many weeks. She remembers John's sister Ethel putting food in front of her; then insisting she eat it. She knows the children were all devastated and she knew she had to try to act normal for their benefit. Ethel was trying to balance her time between her own family, Rebecca's household and her older brother Isaac's home. Isaac was not the oldest. Andrew was, but Isaac had been in very poor health for a really long time, even before John became sick. Everyone had believed Isaac would be the first sibling to pass away. His wife Opal was almost blind and could not care for him. She was very sickly herself. Poor Ethel, she had her own family to tend to and Rebecca knew she was not helping the situation any by not getting a grip on her life. She had to now if for no other reason but for Ethel. So

Rebecca began a prayer ritual. She started by praying every day for the strength to just go on.

Rebecca did not feel old until John died. Now she was feeling about one-hundred and one and as if she needed to die herself. Horrible thoughts would cross her mind like:

"How inconsiderate of John to just die away when he was needed so."
She and the children needed him so badly. She would then beat herself up for her awful thoughts. Some days she was just mad at him for dying. She supposed all of these emotions were normal, but she had a difficult time accepting any of them. She really was not very old and even after having nine children, she was still slim and stood tall. Many would say she was a very beautiful woman. She did not feel pretty anymore. She knew she was hollowed eyed and as pale as a ghost. The Dahl children were born so closely together and the hard farm work must have kept off any weight she should have gained. Now with John's death she was having a real hard time reaching one-hundred pounds.

Since Rebecca stayed very pale, and seemingly weak, her son (Mr. Everett Dahl) had taken it upon himself to stop once again at Doc Browns office. This time Everett's intentions were to have the good doctor check out his mother. So, just as the day when Dr. Brown had made a surprise visit to John, Rebecca was just as surprised when he showed up at her door to check on her. She knew she could not fault her son, as he was much like his mother and often would take a situation into his own hands.

After an examination, the doctor admitted she was fine. He felt the weight loss and the pale
143

skin were caused by all of the problems of this year. He stated that stress had taken its toll on her. Rebecca even admitted to the doctor that sometimes she felt her hair even hurt. Maybe, in the jest of the thought this could have been true because her hair had never been cut. The long hair fell down below her hips by now. She just twisted it up into the bun she always wore and just went on about her daily business. Maybe she should have cut it along the way before marrying into the Dahl family. She was very aware of how the Dahl's felt about a woman and her hair. Some members of the family had gone so far as to say it was a sin for a woman to cut her hair. She was told it was in the Old Testament somewhere, but she had never found that text. Probably because she liked to read the New Testament best and realized she should probably study the Old Testament more.

Rebecca had always heard an old saying that sometimes when one partner dies; the other sometimes dies a short time later. Why if John had to die, why could she just not have died with him? After making that remark to the doctor, she realized how selfish with the showing of self-pity that must have sounded. She already knew the answer to that question before she heard the words come out of the good old doctor's mouth. He told her she had to be strong, not just for herself but for the children. He told her of how John had faith in her and of how she was going to be alright. He told her of how well she and John had raised their children and of how blessed she was to have their help and their precious love. He was so right of course and yes, she knew she had to strengthen-up for her children. Besides, she was sure her health was well. She could tell from the actions of old Doc Brown. He was once again showing that old nervous habit of twisting the chain and pulling out his watch every few minutes. She knew this was because he knew he had to be somewhere else very shortly.

A smile came across Rebecca's face as she thought of how the watch habit of the doctor was a sure sign one was healthy. It is a wonder that old man did not die of hypertension the way he fluttered around with such great speed from one house to another. As Rebecca listened to the doctor friend, she had a silent talk with herself. She knew Dr. Brown did not need to be wasting his time on her. She just had to quit feeling so sorry for herself and quit having these selfish thoughts. So, she prayed about getting her thoughts and body back into working condition. She knew she had to be there for the older children and had to finish raising the little ones. It helped to hear the doctor tell her that John believed in her and that he knew she could do it. So, as she ushered the good doctor out the door, she made up her mind that she was just going to do it!

# Chapter 13

In the year after John's death, Rebecca had toughened up much and she was getting tougher and tougher everyday just out of necessity. She did cry herself to sleep just about every night for a while, but she found a solution for that really quickly. All she had to do was work very hard every minute of the day until she would collapse into the bed. This guaranteed she would sometimes fall asleep before she even hit the pillow. It was those nights she woke up after being asleep that about killed her. She knew she must stay strong in the daylight for the children. This suddenly became her normal routine. The only times she would let herself fall completely apart was in the shadows of her bedroom, in the corner of a barn or somewhere no one would ever see her.

When it came to facing the world, Rebecca had given herself a new rule. She was going to show the world how strong and brave she could be. This was to be her new rule. No one ever needs to feel sorry for her again. She, with the help and the respect of her older children would

147

start running their farm like one would run an army. She expected and got nothing but the very best of work from each and every child. Many decisions were difficult for her to make, but she buckled down and made them. She knew she was going to have to take Dale Henderson out of school before long, which made her feel very badly. Maybe he could continue somewhere later in the future. She figured she would most probably have to take James George out in a couple of years as well. All she could do now was pray that they could each complete their education at some later date.

Elizabeth did get married to her young man Mathew from the neighboring town of Vinton. They had a nice church wedding in March, just two months after John's death. It was hard for everyone but the wedding had been planned for so long and Rebecca insisted they go ahead and get married. John would have wanted this. Everyone was still so hurt and frail. But just like Rebecca, each child had decided to put on his or her strongest face and to hold their heads up high for the whole world to see. She was so very proud of her children. Each showed John's strength. She knew their actions were to help each other as much as showing the community they would survive. She also knew each one of her children had their own secret little break downs just as she, but they set their jaws in a firm manner, held their heads high and proved to the world they would survive.

The wedding was a mixture of happiness and sadness. Elizabeth tried to hold back her tears as she walked down the aisle. As she passed her mother, she whispered,

148

"Father should be walking me down this aisle."

Then she gave John Jr. a big hug. Rebecca could hear her thanking him for taking their fathers place. Tears flowed from everyone. Many tears from the loss of their father's presence and some for the happiness they felt for the handsome young couple as they walked out the door to start their new lives. The couple had purchased that little house and farm they had found months before that was close to Danville. They were going to spend their wedding night in their new home. They were so excited about that. Rebecca knew she was going to miss her daughter completely, but she knew it was time to let her go.

Thank God Everett, still being of a fairly young age, had decided not to be in such a mad rush to get married. Rebecca was very thankful for that decision because his help was still so badly needed at the Dahl farm. If Hazel were there too, he would be too busy with his own family to be of much help to John, Jr. and the others. She and John had been very worried about their wanting to get married at such a young age. She remembered how thankful John was when Mr. Nash had laid down the rules right from the get-go. John had felt Everett and Hazel were both getting too excited too young. Thank God her parents felt the delay was a good idea as well. The couple did however now have a date set and for the moment this seemed to keep them happy.

Rebecca was just as determined to make sure nothing destroyed Everett and Hazel's happiness and that the date they had chosen to be married would be the very date they would marry. They had decided to have a church wedding on

149

September 1st, 1934. The wedding would be held at the Danville church where Hazel and her parents were members. This was now also where Elizabeth and her husband had become new members. John and Rebecca had met Hazel's parents shortly before his passing. Hazel's mother had told them she was going to make Hazel's dress. She stated she would need every day of the extended time to finish the dress Hazel had desired. Hazel had requested her dress have pearl covered buttons from the top of the neck line to way below the waist line, and lots of lace sewn into the full length of the skirt. Rebecca was sure from the sound of the dress design it would be very beautiful. However, she believed it would pale in beauty compared to the beauty of her new daughter-in-law to be. Hazel was a very beautiful young lady.

Life went on as normal as one could expect, but it was as if a black cloud was hanging over the Dahl household. This black cloud had no intention of leaving anytime soon. Although expected, in August of that same year, more trouble came their way. John's sister-in-law died. They lived in a small home that was about a mile from the main road. They had a dirt drive back to the house. Since it was a good way back off the road, Rebecca had offered her home for the viewings. Her home, being on a corner and in a fork of the roads, made so much more sense than using the other family homes. Cars would have had a terrible time getting back that old deep ditched drive. This gave a nice place for the whole family to gather. Ethel volunteered her home as well because she felt Rebecca may not be up to it, but Rebecca insisted. She knew Ethel had been the
150

one who had taken so much care of the brother and sister-in-law and she would still need to tend to her brother. Ethel would cook their meals and kept their house clean all the while she was running her own household. Rebecca felt this was just too much on Ethel.

Remembering the old saying of how when one dies the other may be dead in a year. That old saying must be true, especially when it is the man who is left alone. Or, maybe it was only true in the case where one was in as poor of health as Isaac. The poor man was dead himself by the end of the year.

Rebecca was praying for the year of 1932 to just be over. It sure was not a good year for the Dahl family. Once again Rebecca gave her house for the viewing and once again the wreaths were placed upon her doors. Once again the signs were placed along the roads. Many felt Rebecca had taken on too much by allowing her home to be the viewing yet again. Though not running on full speed to date, she was now showing some of her new found strength. She felt it was the least she could do while knowing that Ethel was surely worn out after taking so much care of the two for so long. Besides, it was her duty as a member of the Dahl family. Somehow she felt John would have wanted her to do as much. Isaac and Opal's deaths were somewhat expected. None the less, it was still very painful for the whole family to lose still another sibling and an in-law just within one year.

No one had made any remarks about the grander dress Beatrice had picked out for Rebecca to wear to John's funeral. She felt now that the attendees would be more of the Dahl's and less of

151

her family. She should now find something a little more religious. She would have never agreed to wear that dress had she been in control of herself. She was thankful at least Beatrice had made sure she looked her very best for her last visit with John. Once again she found herself going to those old trunks for something to wear. She found an old dark green velvet dress that had long sleeves. It had a high neckline and was not so tight around waist. This dress was much more modest than that form fitting black suit-dress. Being the age of the dress, it did flow to a full length, but Rebecca was getting pretty good with the needle by now. She hemmed it up to about the middle of her legs. This had become the style somewhere in the teens or the twenties and was still the style by now. Seven petticoats were no longer needed, you made due with only one. Rebecca knew her redesigning of this dress would make it look more acceptable to the local and farm people. She figured maybe no one would pay too much attention to the expensive hand designed ivory colored lace that came up high onto the sleeves as a cuff. Nor would they notice too much the neckline that was covered in a wide stripe of the same lace and pearls. She was hoping none of these Quaker type people would feel it was prideful to own such a thing.

While searching through the ole trunks, Rebecca had found a green felt hat that matched the dress fairly well. It had many pretty colored stones and pearls around the rim of it. It had several ostrich feathers standing up on one side from the rim, but over the years the glue had let loose on several of the feathers and some of the stones. She was glad of that because it made them
152

come off easier. This would have been way too fancy for her to wear. So she took off all the pretties and used some of the material from the bottom of her dress to sew as a band over the rim. This covered all of the glue spots. She was amazed as to how nice the changes became and this certainly brought the outfit together. It made a mighty decent looking hat if she did say so herself. Now she had a proper funeral attire that fit in with the community in which she now lived. She wore this ensemble to both Opal's and now Isaac's funerals.

During Isaac's funeral, Rebecca started her doubting questioning stuff once again. She was feeling so sorry for John's family. His family seemed to be as doomed as hers had been so many years ago. Why, she wondered? This family was a good family. They attended church three or more times per week or every chance they got. They worked hard from daylight until they could not see any more at night. They were good honest people and they prayed and thanked God every day for what little they had. Why were they being punished? She was going to have to get over these feelings once again. There was a passage in the bible that said,

"It is appointed unto man once to die."
But little thoughts would pass through her mind thinking of how the appointments could have been spread out a little. Of how God could have at least let them catch their breath between funerals. She felt shameful for her thoughts because not one of the Dahl family members ever made such remarks as she. Her remarks were usually just in her mind, but she felt guilty just the same. Instead of complaining, she could hear in the Dahl family
153

prayers of how thankful they were that God had given them the time He had with each one of their loved ones. This made Rebecca think her thoughts must be sinful. Very sinful indeed! This beautiful family was so thankful, just very humble and so very thankful. They were forever thanking God. No matter what happened to them, they all just seemed to thank God.

Rebecca loved this family so very much. She knew they lived by a passage in the Bible that told of how one was supposed to count their many blessings every day. She knew that she must study her Bible more. She was not even sure if that was an actual passage or maybe words to a song. She just wasn't sure. Today she wished she could have been more like the Dahl's. She wanted to pray that God would give her the same kind of faith and hope the wonderful Dahl family lived by each and every day of their lives. It seemed to work for them. They seemed so much stronger than most people. Then another thought passed her mind. Were the Dahl's now just hardened from so much grief? No, that could not be the case. She had not hardened yet. So, it is possible that no one is ever even half way prepared to lose someone they love to a death.

# C hapter 14

Christmas was sad this year. John Jr. was wonderful. He had taken over the role of his father with the smaller children. With Everett and Mabel's help, he got all the excitement built up for the gathering of a tree. Rebecca made the chocolate milk as usual and everyone carried on the family tradition. She knew John Jr. and some of the others were just going through the motions, but she also knew that was very necessary for the younger children.

Elizabeth had planned on coming home, but it snowed badly. To add to the disappointments of life, she was unable to come. Her husband had been worried about making the trip because they were expecting their first child. It was due sometime in January.

Gwen did not get to come home again this year either. This time it was of her own making. She had chosen to wait to come home after her first niece or nephew was born. In her letters she mentioned she had worked out a deal with the hospital to where if she worked week-ends for three months at a time then they, the hospital administration, would give her a full month off at one time. She liked this idea, and wrote of how nice it was of the hospital to agree to do such a thing for her. Then she added,

"You know they allowed these concessions simply because my family lives so far 'Down in the Hills'!"

She had placed a 'Ha! Ha!' at the end of her statement in her normal Gwen joking fashion. She now planned to come home for the month of March 1933.

Christmas came and went. The children seemed to really enjoy the little gifts everyone had put together for them. Different people of the community had gathered items together to help this year. Things like hand me down winter coats and a few toys. The children did not seem to notice if an item was new or old. Rebecca baked her applesauce cake. This was a very big hit with the whole family. She made an extra one for Ethel's family. Her heart was warmed when she looked into the seating room to see Mabel sitting on the floor with all the family members around her. She was reading a book about the night of Christmas. Everyone was smiling and she could see a glimmer in each child's eye.

On January 26th a precious little boy was born to Rebecca's daughter Elizabeth. Rebecca had worried about leaving her children for any length of time, but Mabel had insisted she and her brothers could take very good care of the little ones. Mabel told Rebecca she knew Aunt Ethel would be checking in on them anyway. So, after a little persuasion, Rebecca went on to Elizabeth's about a week before the birth of her grandson. This timing worked out just right. Elizabeth knew the due date was near that week, so Rebecca just went ahead to take care of her daughter. At that time she of course did not know how long she would have to stay before the baby was born. It was just sheer luck he was born less than a week after her arrival.

Rebecca had ridden with Everett while he was on one of his visits to see Hazel. He visited for a while with his sister. Long enough to make fun of how fat she had become. He kept asking if she was sure there was a baby in there or had she just been unable to refuse that last biscuit. Recanting his words by saying,

"No, that couldn't be it, because I forgot you can't cook."
This went on until Rebecca laughingly said he must stop picking on his sister that way. He left only after Elizabeth told him she could not laugh anymore because it was hurting her side. He hugged his sister, did sort of an air kick and off he went. He blew a kiss to his mother as he breezed by her. She screamed for him to please be careful. After visiting with his girlfriend, he was to head back home by himself. This worried Rebecca because this would be unlike all the other times when she had waited up to see that he got home safely. This time she would not have any way of knowing.

Putting aside all the joking, Elizabeth had become huge and looked like she would surely pop any minute. On the day of the birth, the doctor they had called seemed to be very slow in coming. Rebecca, being of impatience, worried and wished she had just brought Doctor Brown along. Of course she knew he could not have come that far, but he she trusted. However, the
157

other doctor did arrive in time and delivered an eight-pound, five-ounce bouncing baby boy. His name was to be Simon. The husband's hair was of a very dark brown and Elizabeth's hair had always been toe blonde. Elizabeth had taken her hair color from her Auntie Beatrice. Simon had the heaviest head of black hair, really black hair. In the two weeks Elizabeth stayed after his birth, she found his hair to be curly as well. This caused great relieve as he had at least inherited something from his mother.

What a beautiful child little Simon was. Rebecca laughed at herself when a thought crossed her mind that she was now truly a Dahl. Because she just kept catching herself saying,

"Thank you Jesus, Thank you Lord."

Yes, God givith and God takith away. Oh, how she wished John could have seen their beautiful first grandchild. She knew he would have loved him so very much. All of a sudden something wonderful had happened to this family and instead of being sad, Rebecca caught herself smiling all the time. She would even smile when she thought of John. She remembered the big smile John would get when he realized one of their children was a boy. She remembered how he would prance around the house like he was the only person who had done something wonderful by creating a boy. She also could remember the tenderness and the pride he had with the birth of every girl. Simon was wonderful and exciting to have for many reasons. He was like the healing this big family needed so badly. Life and death were like the four seasons. A baby's birth was as if it was spring.

Like all wonderful things, they have to come to an end. The Sunday arrived when

158

Rebecca had to go home. Before leaving for home, Elizabeth and her husband took Simon to church for the first time. It was sort of a show off day. All the members of that church thought he was one of the prettiest babies they had ever seen. Rebecca already knew that without being told. The Nash's were very excited to see the new baby and to have Rebecca come to their church. They already felt like they were family and Rebecca was very pleased to see Hazel again. She reached over and put her hand on Everett's arm and said,

"Good-morning Son."

She was told that Everett and Hazel always sat way back towards the back of the church on most Sunday's, but today they had chosen to sit with Everett's family. Rebecca smiled and said,

"Shouldn't we feel honored."

Everyone seemed to be in a tug of war to hold the baby. They must have worn him out as somehow he ended up asleep in Hazel's arms. Hazel held Simon throughout the remainder of the service. Rebecca could not help but notice she too would be a great mother. She understood why she liked Hazel so much.

The Nash family was so nice. After the service, they invited everyone to come to their house for dinner. Rebecca told them she hated to decline but she had already prepared a meal for today at Elizabeth's. She stated also that since she was going home with Everett that evening after he and Hazel had attended the evening service, she had best spend the rest of her day to pack up.

Rebecca was happy to be going home, though hating to leave her beautiful new grand-baby and daughter. She had missed her other children so badly. This was the first time *ever* she

159

had been away from the little ones. It was nice to spend those days with one of her children and with her new grandchild, but it was also nice to be going home. All the way home Everett gloated about how handsome his little new nephew was. He completely dismissed the fact that the baby's father had black hair. He kept saying how much Simon looked just like him. Everett had the darkest hair of all the boys. It was also curly, thus giving him what he thought, bragging rights over his new nephew.

Rebecca and John had raised their children not to boast, so she believed the biggest part of his verbiage was all in a teasing manner. Everett then became a mite concerned when he thought of James being the baby boy of the family. He kept asking his mother things like,

"Do you think James will be jealous, or do you think he will love him?"

She laughed at the rambling of her son but thought about it for a second and realized she just was not sure about that one herself. All she knew was with everything the children had gone through; Simon was a wonderful breath of fresh air. The little guy did not know how badly he was needed to bring this family out of their dark distress. She smiled to herself and thought he was just what the doctor ordered.

# C hapter 15

The first day of March brought the much awaited visit from Gwen. Surprisingly, it was pretty and a sun shiny winter day. John Jr. was busy on the farm as usual, so he sent Everett to Gallipolis to pick up Gwen. Dale Henderson wanted to tag along. Everett said he did not care if Mother agreed. Then James George wanted to go. Rebecca said,

"Okay."

She then laughed and said to the little girls,

"Oh, shucks, why don't you two just go along as well, Gwen can just sit on your lap."

As Everett was leaving, the children just kept jumping into the car. Rebecca knew Gwen would be happy about all the fuss, but could not help but wonder where they would put her. Before it was all over, the only ones to stay at home were Rebecca and John, Jr.

Rebecca was so anticipating the joy of this visit. She stayed in the kitchen the biggest part of the day as she cooked all of Gwen's favorite dishes. She had also made a blue scarf for her. She had worked on it until really late last night. Robin blue was her daughter's favorite color. By

161

now Gwen had sent home many beautiful poems. Rebecca had picked out her favorite poem and had embroidered it on the scarf. She smiled with her thoughts of how that girl should have been a poet instead of a nurse. More beautiful poetry Rebecca had never seen. She wondered where that talent had come from. She did not believe it came from her side of the family. Yet, none of the Dahl's seemed to have that kind of talent either. Many could play some sort of an instrument, but never had she heard of anyone writing poetry. She laughed to herself when she thought of how she felt she could not make two words sound good together on paper. Maybe it came from further back in her family. She would have liked to take a little credit for these smart children. Hey, then again, many in her family were newspaper reporters. Of course that is nothing like writing poetry she supposed. So she just didn't know if she could claim Gwen's talents. She let out a chuckle and looked out of the window to see the children pulling back into the driveway.

As the Model T pulled up the driveway, Rebecca could feel the excitement of finally seeing her beloved daughter. It had been so long. The doors flew open as each child stepped out of the car. The excitement was building up in Rebecca today. She was in such a wonderful mood. She laughed out loud again when she said to herself,

"Did I really have that many children?"
A beautiful young lady who was only a child it seemed like only yesterday, stepped out. First you saw a stocking leg with a very pretty black high heeled shoe. Then came what looked like a high fashioned gal from a magazine. She was dressed

162

in all her finery. That beautiful shiny black hair had been cut into a new style.

Rebecca never was quite sure where that pretty black hair had come from, but it was flowing loosely below her hat. She guessed that was the style now of days. Someone had told her it was called a 'Bob'. Whatever it may be called, it certainly looked beautiful on her daughter. Rebecca felt all of her children were most beautiful, but in her heart she knew Gwen was the drop dead gorgeous one. There just could not be anyone on earth any prettier than her. Gwen was one beautiful young lady. Rebecca would bet every man in that big old city whom ever came in contact with her would try for her hand in marriage. Of course Rebecca would never hear about those sorts of things if that were the case. Gwen was so closed mouth about her personal life.

Happy times seemed to be coming back to the Dahl family. Everyone was home. Elizabeth was close enough to visit on some weekends or even just for a Sunday. Gwen, of course fell in love with Simon the minute she laid eyes upon him. He must have waited to show off for his Aunt Gwen because the first time she picked him up, he gave her a great big smile. One could see her just melt with love for this precious new baby.

James, whom they all had believed might be a little jealous, was instead elated with his new nephew. This had worried everyone because Elizabeth had always been like another mother to James. He was so very special to her. They had felt maybe if it were a girl he would handle it a little better, but their worries were all unfounded because he was so happy and proud to be an uncle. If anyone was jealous at all, it was Bella. She

163

showed some signs of jealousy. Every one guessed this was probably understandable as Elizabeth had doted on her just as she had James and Edith. Since Simon was a boy, no one had really thought of her being jealous before. She was such a pleasant child and jealousy was very out of character for her. Bella was always the one who could entertain herself better than any of the other children had ever done. As soon as Elizabeth realized Bella's dismay, she picked her up and any little jealousy pains she may have had seemed to be solved once Elizabeth put her upon her lap. While others were holding Simon, Elizabeth talked to Bella about the new baby and of how she was now a big girl and an aunt. This made Simon her baby too and that seemed to make everything okay. She also realized she still had a big place in her big sister's heart.

Ever chance the family got during the month of March, they spent it with Elizabeth and the baby. The plans were for the little family to visit the Dahl household so they could all go as a family to their home church the last Sunday of March. This was the Sunday before Gwen was to leave to go home. Everyone, including the extended Dahl family members was dying to see the new baby. Weather permitting, this had been the plan. Gwen was to leave to go back to Columbus, Ohio that following Tuesday.

March in Ohio is usually very cold. One morning during that last week of Gwen's visit, the family awakened to do the chores as usual. They found it was pouring down rain. This was a wet, cold rain. Gwen in her poetic voice said,

"It is pouring buckets of rain and mother cannot scream for anyone still asleep this morning.
164

She will be lost as to what to say, unless of course you would like to hear her say, 'Arise', you little heathens you missed a bucket full of rain!"

They all laughed knowing their mother's favorite saying was,

"Rise and Shine! You're Burning Sunshine."

Or,

"Everybody up! You are Burning Sunshine."

All of the children loved repeating their mother's favorite saying in jest. They knew just how far they could go with that however, because their mother was always very serious when she would say these things. When they knew she would accept it well, and as a joke, they would tease her on how she would always get that last phrase into her sentence.

Rain or no rain, chores had to be done. Finally the children and their mother had completed all their tasks. Just as everyone had finally dried off some and were ready to sit down for breakfast, one of the boys who was sitting by the window saw some cows where they were not supposed to be. John Jr. rushed back outside into the rain to review the situation. This family had been raised to work very hard and never questioned the things they had to do to survive. Rebecca had found a new strength by this time and was ruling over her family with an iron hand. She never looked at it that way until she overheard Mabel telling a friend that,

"Her mother ruled their family with an iron hand."

This hurt for a moment, but she then realized it was not meant to hurt her. It was only meant to

165

show her children were very proud of her for having the strength to take control after John's death.

John Jr. came running back through the door just as fast as he could and screamed,

"The cattle are out!"

When this sort of thing happened, no one messed around even a second. From the largest to the smallest, they hustled to get their boots on and out the door they ran. Rebecca got everything off of the stove and followed in a rush behind her children.

Rebecca started managing the situation. She screamed in a loud voice,

"Move it! Get those cattle back into that field before they get into the neighbors barnyard!"

No one complained. Poor little James must have gotten the wrong boots as he kept stepping down into his rubbers while trying to keep up with everyone. All the while he was trying to keep on those boots. He had them half on and half off. Rebecca felt so sad for her littlest of sons. He is still just a baby, she thought. Just a little over ten years old, but he has to become a man now. He must become a man without a father. She could feel the tears swell up into her eyes as she watched him dragging a sleeve of his coat while trying to button it on the run and still trying to keep those boots on his feet. Did he complain? Not one complaining word came out of that little boy's mouth! Things like this did hurt Rebecca very badly, but what was she to do. He was a strong headed little youngster and he was going to show the world he could do anything they could do. This little guy forged ahead with a determination of a man, knowing in his little heart that he could not get behind or he would get left.

Within an hour the fences were repaired and the cattle were safe inside the Dahl property. All milking and feeding had already been done. The family was just sitting around the table or drying off by their potbellied stove. The boys were waiting for their mother, Mabel and Gwen to reheat breakfast.

Breakfast at the Dahl home was something to behold. Although they were usually the same, it was always a spread that looked like a feast. They always had country ham from the cellar house. It was cut into big and thick slices. It was then browned just right. They always had homemade biscuits that they covered with cow's home churned butter. They had canned jellies and jams. Mother always fixed chunked potatoes with the skins still on them, and they were fried. Along with this they had plenty of eggs fixed in every way possible. There were some that were sunny side up. There were some scrambled and there were some fried thin as paper with crushed edges around them. Rebecca did these things because of the children's different choices. They always had lots of homemade gravy to go with all of that. Due to the plenteousness of farm living and the hard work put into that farm, the Dahl family never went hungry.

It was midmorning by now and some of the children said they were starving to death by the time they got to sit back down at the table. Gwen remarked that by city standards, this was still very early. Breakfast at the Dahl's was usually over by 6:30 or 7:00 a.m. She told her family of how just now city folk would be getting up to start their

167

day. Everyone laughed in disbelief. Everett said loudly,

"Those must be some lazy folks up there."

After breakfast, as the girls and Rebecca were cleaning the kitchen, Gwen stopped and leaned up against a cabinet for a short time. John, Jr. was sitting at the table where he had already started separating some dried fruit for the children to have later. He noticed what was happening and he jumped up to catch Gwen just as she was leaning backwards to fall. Rebecca had her back towards them, because she was washing the dishes and did not see Gwen's weakness. John, Jr. spoke up and said,

"Mother, at the risk of scaring you, Gwen about passed out."

He added,

"Not to worry you mother or to be a tattle tale, but she did the very same thing after running across that back field a while ago. I had to catch her out there too. She must be sick!"

He looked at her pale face and exclaimed,

"She is sick mother, look at her. She is as white as a ghost!"

Gwen did not make any complaints when John, Jr. recommended that they put her to bed. Rebecca wasted no time following that suggestion. She dried off her hands on her apron and grabbed Gwen's other arm and they lead her to Rebecca's bedroom. This room was downstairs. Putting her there was the best idea since she did not look as if she could climb any stairs.

Once Gwen was in the bedroom and covered up in the bed, Rebecca ask her what she believed was wrong. She replied with,

"Nothing mother!"

Then she just lay there staring at her mother through those dark piercing eyes. Finally, she said,

"Mother, please don't worry about me. I am just having my monthly and it seems to be taking its toll on me this month."

Rebecca was relieved and kissed Gwen on her forehead. She then pulled the covers clear up around her daughter's neck, leaving only her mouth and eyes above the covers while saying,

"Get some rest angel."

As Rebecca walked out, she stood at the door a minute just watching her beautiful daughter and praying that this was all that was wrong with her. Gwen flashed those dark eyes at her mother as if in anger and said,

"Really mother, don't you have enough to worry about without worrying over a sissy city woman while she is having what nature calls normal? I am just cold and damp, once I get warm I will be okay! I promise!"

The whole day passed without Gwen getting up. She hadn't even moved much. She just never did get out of bed. Everyone in the family made at least one pass by the bedroom door during the day to check on her. She was so soundly asleep and no one wanted to trouble her by waking her. After the feeding and gathering of the eggs that evening, the family sit down for dinner. At this time Rebecca decided it was time Gwen was awakened and called to the table to eat. She went into the darken bedroom and sit down on the bed with her daughter. She pushed the dark hair away from her face while she was still asleep. The minute she let her hand touch Gwen's face she knew something was definitely wrong. She placed
169

her hand upon her forehead, only to find her daughter was burning up with a fever. She said to herself,

"'Okay!' Now Rebecca you can worry!"
She ran out of the bedroom to get John, Jr. She found him and told him in a scared voice to run to Vinton and find Dr. Brown immediately! She then stated,

"Gwen has the worst fever I have ever encountered!"
She then told Mabel to get chilled water and some wet towels. They simply must bring that fever down.

It seemed like hours before old Doc Brown walked through that door. John had told him of the urgently and he had just stepped into the Dahl's Model T while leaving his own vehicle at home. So in reality the three miles could not have taken as long as Rebecca believed it to be. Rebecca had tried over and over to arouse Gwen, but to no avail. Dr. Brown checked her temperature and said it was way too high. He asked if there was any alcohol in the house. Rebecca said yes! He then told Mabel and Rebecca to strip her and bath her in alcohol. He would visit with the others while they did that.

About one hour after bathing Gwen, she began to regain consciousness. They did not know whether the results were from the bath or from a shot Doc Brown had given her. After everyone calmed down and Gwen seemed to be okay, the doctor got up to go home. As he was getting back into the Model T, he stepped back out of the car for a second time showing a concern upon his face. He said,

170

"Rebecca, you bring that young lady into my office just as soon as she is ready to ride."
Then he added,

"I do not like the color of her skin. She is too sick to just have a cold, flu or her monthly as she would like us to believe."
He then said something about not wanting to cause her any extra concern; however he would feel better if he could check her more thoroughly just to be sure she was okay. Then he mumbled something about how one could probably catch about anything from living in that nasty old city.

Tuesday came and went and needless to say, Gwen was not able to go home on schedule. Rebecca drafted a letter to her employment telling them of her illness and of how she could not return until she was well. Two days passed with Gwen gaining very little strength. On the third day, John pulled the Model T up to the front of the porch so they could load her easily. She was just a tiny little thing and John, Jr. could have just picked her up the same as picking up a bag of feed. While playing around, he had done that very thing many of a time, but Gwen was so weak at this point he wanted to be safe. She was so weak to where they were even taking her to the doctor's office in her gown, her slippers and a night jacket. She didn't even put up much of a protest to that matter. Being of such a proud nature, one was surprised she did not put up a fuss.

During the examination, Rebecca and John, Jr. walked around in the waiting room wondering what on earth could be wrong. Rest assured they were worried! They were both very worried. Neither took a seat. They both felt something seemed terribly wrong. Rebecca felt bad after she
171

had asked John, Jr. just how much he thought this kind of an examination, in the doctor's office was going to cost. John, Jr., had just hung his head and said,

"Lots, mother! It will probably be lots."
After what seemed to be hours, Dr. Brown came through the door of the waiting room. He looked ashen as he said,

"John, would you give me a few minutes with your mother?"
As John, Jr. left the room he felt a cold feeling go down his spine, wondering what could be wrong. Then he thought, Oh God, this is very serious. He knew this to be true by the way the doctor was acting.

John, Jr. had not prayed much lately. He guesses he had been too busy trying to keep mother from losing her mind and keeping as much sanity as he could in his entire family. He stepped around the building and did everything in his power to keep from crying. He knew he was now definitely the man of the house. If it is something serious, if she needs an operation or anything, he felt the need to tell his mother and Gwen not to worry. They would do whatever that had to be done. If anyone worried about the money, he would just plant an extra field of grain this year and take it to the market. He could surly work out something with Doctor Brown. After all, he was a friend of their family. They could probably make payments to the nice old gentleman. The only fact in John, Jr.'s mind right now was to be sure his mother and sister did not worry.

John, Jr. found a corner of the building outside of the doctor's office. He had never noticed this private little spot before. He found
172

himself kneeling to the ground as he started to pray.

"Dear God, mother cannot take anymore. We have had so much these past days. Please let Gwen get well."

He prided himself to being a brave strong man, but he could feel hot tears forming in the corner of his eyes. He was always closest to Gwen. They were buddies and had been all of their lives. She was born just a little under two years after him. Thoughts kept racing through his mind as he was telling himself,

"Be brave John Dahl. You are a man, and you must be brave, if in no other way, at least in front of mother and Gwen. You must be strong!"

As he was getting up from that position, he felt a very sharp pain in his stomach. Ah Ha! He thought! We all have a virus! I'm probably catching it too. Well I, for one, don't have time to get sick, he thought. He smiled with relief believing Gwen probably just got a stomach virus and caught the flu while catching those cattle the other day. That day was a very cold rainy day. Those dang cattle! Maybe he should have checked those fences more often.

After a short time of talking with himself, and convincing himself on the flu idea and of his bravery, John saw his mother coming out of the door. He noticed right away that she had been crying. All of his thoughts and hopes vanished in a flash. All of a sudden he felt the worst sinking feeling inside. Oh God it is serious, it is very serious! Mother said nothing. Dear God! Was it so bad she couldn't even speak of it? All she said was,

"John, please go in and get your sister."

Her voice seemed to just fade away as she completed her sentence saying that the doctor had said we can take her home now. All the way home there was nothing but complete silence. John, Jr. looked over at Gwen, who looked back at him with those dark eyes surrounded by skin as white as her gown. He could tell by the redness of her eyes that she too had been crying.

Upon their arrival at home, they put Gwen back into the bed. Once again into mother's bed. John wanted to ask questions, but he knew he had to get the children moving to complete their chores before dark. Once the chores were done and he returned to the house, he saw that Gwen was sound asleep. He noticed that mother was missing. He realized it was getting dark so he went back outside looking for her. As he walked past the old corn shed, he could hear whimpers. He could hear a soft prayer coming from his mother's mouth. He just froze in his steps, not meaning to listen but he could not help himself. He heard her begging God. He had never heard such begging in his life, much less coming from his mother's mouth. She was praying,

"Please God, Please Dear God, Oh God, don't take my daughter. Lord, you have taken my parents, my husband, many of his family members who were dear to me and so many loved ones from me."

Her voice rose as she asked,

"What have I done to deserve this? Just tell me what I have done? What can I do for you to spare me yet another loss of another part of my very soul? I know you givith and you takith away, but Lord have I not givith enough? I know we all

174

belong to you, and I know I am not supposed to question you, but my baby? Lord, my baby!"
Then she almost screamed,

"Dear Lord, why do you have to take my baby?"

John, Jr. took a few more steps because he was feeling guilty for listening to his mother's prayer, but he could feel what felt like a big rock go to the very pit of his being. He could hardly hold his legs still as the realization hit on what the doctor must have told his mother. It was soaking in like a raging river. It felt like a sledge hammer slowly moving from his ears to each section of his body, pounding one inch at a time. He thought he was going to fall down.

"Oh No! Oh no, Gwen is going to die! Dear God, Gwen is going to die!"

Gwen was dying, he heard that part loud and clear and that had to be the problem.

"Dear God, what were they going to do?"
He stood their quietly. He had to because his feet now felt like lead. He was frozen to that spot as he heard his mother pray for a good long while. Then she would just cry for a while. It was one of those earth-shattering cries. One might call it that death sounding whimper. The one to where someone could not cry anymore and their body and voice were just making sounds and movements. Whimpers and shakes. He wanted so badly to just go to his mother and tell her that he had heard and hoped that may ease her pain. Could he maybe comfort her? He did not know what to do. It didn't matter much anyway as he was sure he could not move from the spot he was frozen in. He needed someone to comfort him right now too, because he was in complete shock.

175

Just as John seemed to get the feeling back into his legs and had the intention of going to his mother, he noticed she had changed from a prayer to a conversation. It sounded as if she was now talking to his father. She was talking just as if he were still there. Once again, John, Jr. found himself frozen to his spot and was just listening. Sometimes it would sound as though she was mad at his father. She would ask him how he could have gone away and left her to deal with so much of this horrible pain, leaving her all alone. Then you could hear her whimper,

"Please, please, please, dear God, please!"
He then realized it would be worse to bother her. He was not sure he could manage any encouragement himself. He was going to pieces inside as he knew he was not handling the news with any great strength. He must compose himself before ever even thinking of talking with mother.

John, Jr. knew he must get back into the house before some of the children would worry and maybe follow him! There is no way another child should hear this news in this way. He now must clear up his own face before walking back in that direction. He let the tears flow a while longer, big man or not. How could they bear any more pain? He felt his weakness when it came to the thoughts of losing his sister, so how was he going to be of any help to anyone else. He just kept whispering,

"Dear God, please take this burden from us! Please give me strength!"
He felt so very helpless as he walked back toward the house. His thoughts were wondering of how bad things could happen to such good people. He believed his mother was probably the nearest thing
176

to perfect God had ever put upon this earth. Why would He allow her to endure such pain? And Gwen, what had she ever done wrong to offend anyone in her short life. Mother had lost just about everyone she ever loved except for her children and now God was going to take one of them.

It seemed to be common knowledge that the loss of a child was even harder than the loss of a husband or wife. A child, a mother had lay down in the jaws of death and delivered it into the world. In his mother's case, she had cherished and loved this child for almost twenty-one years. Gwen was still only twenty. She would be twenty-one on May the 18th. Being as young as she was; how could she be this sick? Now, something was terribly wrong, John realized that Doc Brown had told his mother that Gwen was going to die. He kept saying those words over and over to himself.

"Gwen is going to die! Gwen is going to die!"
Although he had not been much of a praying person, he spread his arms wide open and he threw his hands to the sky and prayed. He begged with every fiber of his body. He prayed all the way to the house, begging,

"Please God take this cup of death from us."

John knew he must now show signs of strength for his mother as well as for Gwen and the other children. Just as he was arriving at the door, he tried to make himself a promise. He promised himself that he would never marry and have children. He decided if you don't have anything to lose, then you cannot lose it. Another promise was to gain the strength to be a good pillar of strength for his mother and Gwen.

As John, Jr. opened the door, he found James pulling on the dress of one of his younger sister's dolls. He screamed,

"James, you stop that this instant!"
John knew he had snapped at his little brother too sharply. He had also, in a loud voice, ordered him straight to bed. Before this night, James had never been so harshly corrected by John, Jr. So, the little lad ran upstairs while crying loudly. John felt like a very big heel at this point because he knew he was James George's idol. Now he had just hurt his feelings more than he would have if he had punished him with a spanking. Guilt caused John to take off upstairs after the little boy and he apologized to him for being so very harsh. He told him of how he was not to tear up any of his sister's things. He told him of how that was very wrong, but he also told him he was sorry he had screamed at him.

Shortly after the little episode with James George, John, Jr. got Mabel to help him put all of the other children to bed. Mabel being aggravated with John for the way she had heard him treating James, rebelled with statements like,

"What is going on with you? It's awfully early, you know. Are you just some kind of an old grump tonight, or what?"
She had given him a very dirty look when he had screamed at James George. Now she considered the time John had chosen for bedtime was completely out of line. She hatefully questioned what was wrong with him. He reminded himself that he had not officially been told anything, so he

178

blurted out something he later felt sounded really stupid,

"No one has told me anything! What makes you think something is wrong!"

John Jr. knew his mother needed no extra stress at this minute and she would tell them all in her own time. So he just needed to blow out the fuse in this situation. He apologized to Mabel and said he was sorry. He told her of how he must be extra tired tonight or something similar. He wasn't exactly sure of what he said. He also told her that mother had taken a walk. Mabel did not rebel to that, as she knew mother often did those sorts of things since father's death. She then agreed it was a good idea to get the children ready for bed. Noticing the stress on John's face, she sang a little song to them instead of reading a book tonight.

The following morning and every day after, during that week, John noticed his mother was in deep prayers and could see a deep sadness cover her face. There were dark bags under her eyes. Should he tell her that he knew? Would that relieve some of this burden she was carrying? No, he decided she would tell him in her own good time.

From that day on, everyone got involved in caring for Gwen. It became apparent she was not returning to work. Different ones would take her meals to her. These meals, she would hardly touch. Even if she did not eat, this helped cause everyone to busy themselves with at least fluffing up her pillows. By this time Mabel had stated to John, Jr. that she knew something was terribly wrong with Gwen, but she too had decided mother would tell them in due time.

Mother and her sister-in-law Ethel often had long talks. The older children were thankful their mother had such a loving sister-in-law and a friend. She needed Aunt Ethel badly during these times. On one of the trips to see Hazel, Everett had stopped and had a talk with Elizabeth. He had told her he felt something was terribly wrong at home. Everett had been questioning John Jr. John kept telling him no one had said anything. Elizabeth decided she must go see about her family. So, she and her family came to visit the very next Sunday, unannounced.

A shock came over everyone when Rebecca would not let them into the house. She said Gwen's illness could not be good for the baby. So everyone had to sit out in the yard and visit. Elizabeth talked with Gwen through a window. Now, it was obvious! This visit made it very clear to those who were old enough to understand that something was terribly wrong with Gwen! At this time the older children all realized the seriousness of the situation. They still had to guess, but they were aware Gwen had some horrible disease.

Before they left, Rebecca called Elizabeth to a corner of the yard and you could see as they were talking, this was a very serious conversation. They hugged, and as they turned their backs to everyone else, you could tell that they were both crying. As Elizabeth got into their car, she hugged Mabel, Everett and John Jr. She whispered to John,

"I told her she has to tell you and the others all about Gwen, and she has agreed to do so. Be brave, it is awful John, it is so awful."

180

With a whitened face and a horribly sad look, Elizabeth just kept saying as they started to drive away,

"It's just awful! It's just awful John!"

The following Sunday, the minister from the church came to the house to see Gwen. He prayed long and hard over Gwen. After he left, Gwen seemed so much more cheerful and almost as if she was getting well. John Jr., knowing how hard it was going to be for mother to tell him or the other children, got brave enough to ask questions of his now healthier sister. As he approached the room, he found just about everyone else in the room as well. Gwen was sitting up and reading her latest poems to the children. He looked at his sister and said,

"We need to have a talk."

He tried to gently remove the other children from the room by telling them if they stepped out for a while for him and Gwen to talk about something, they could come right back and hear a brand new poem Gwen would write before they got back. He looked at Gwen and winked. She agreed.

After everyone had left the room, John pulled up a wooden straight back chair. He wrapped his long legs around the back of it, sitting the wrong way. As he slid the chair up close to the bed, he said,

"Okay Sis, let's talk. Mother is devastated and walking around like we live in a morgue. I am now the head of this household, yet she does not tell me what is going on. I know you are very sick, but I do not know what is wrong with you. Please tell me. I have a right to know."

Gwen lifted her thin white hand, which was holding a lace handkerchief. She put her hand up to his face and she said,

"My dear, sweet brother, I am going to die!"

John Jr. knew this, but to hear his precious sister tell him in so many words was like a brick building just falling upon him. Gwen went on to tell John of how Doctor Brown had told her that obviously from working at the sanatorium with the TB patients, she had acquired the germ of tuberculosis. Getting wet in the rain on that day the cattle got out was a turning point in her condition. She softly whispered while telling him of how that had hastened her destiny. She told him of how she had been walking around with the germ for a long time, but did not know it until she got sick from being wet and cold. That triggered that germ somehow and started the process of full blown tuberculosis. Gwen then said,

"I wanted to tell you, but mother is taking it so badly and I am afraid if anyone shows her any sympathy, she will completely crumble into pieces."

Poor Gwen, she sounded as though she was not sorry about dying. She was sorrier for hurting her mother so badly. Gwen continued,

"She's not sleeping you know? She comes into this room at least fifteen times every night. She does not know I know she is here. She prays over me ever so softly, I know at least once on the hour. John, I have accepted my death. I know it must be God's will and I will be with our father. I miss him so much. Please do not worry about me. We will all be there some day and I am told Heaven is a wonderful place to be."

182

John felt that terrible knot in his stomach again. His nerves were killing him lately. How could his sister be so matter of fact about her own death? Especially when she is not even twenty-one yet. He was second born after Elizabeth, and Gwen was third, which put her just two years younger than he. They had always been so close. They were each other's best friends through all of these years. He had missed her so badly when she was away at work. Now she was going away forever. He got up from his chair and just stood there while his heart broke right in half. He had always heard of a heart break, but today he could really feel his breaking. He could not find any words to say to his beautiful, brave sister. All he could do was kiss her with much affection on the cheek and say.

"I love you Gwen."
He then made a fast dash for the door before he broke down in front of her.

John, Jr. just started walking as fast as he could, past the barns out through the fields. He walked very, very fast and hard around the entire property. He walked as if demons were on his heels. After he had walked or run in a mad haste, he settled down some, but his heart was racing.

"Oh God, what is happening to my family?" thought John, while he hunted for a place of privacy. No matter where he went he felt as if someone was watching. He felt the trees were watching him cry. He made it back to one of the barns where he found a dark corner and just collapsed. He put his head between his legs and cried and cried until he was sure there were no more tears left within his body. His whole body was shaking from sheer grief. He thought of how

183

he was going to have to learn to pray like mother, and the way he had heard father pray while he was alive. All the time thinking maybe if he prayed harder and more often, just maybe God would have spared his loving sister. He got up into a kneeling position, at which time he started his conversation with God. All of a sudden he felt a sharp pain within his stomach. It was so sharp that he let out a mournful cry and doubled over. He heard a noise and realized he was not alone.

Dale Henderson came running up to him. He and James had been playing in the loft of the barn, unbeknownst to their big brother. John knew he must look a fright as he had cried now for a couple of hours. The pain he just had was showing on his face as well. Dale took one look at his brother and said,

"I'm going to get mother,"
as he took James by the hand and begun to run out of the barn towards the house. John Jr. gathered all the strength he could possibly gain and ran after the boys, while mustering up all the speed he could to catch them. Just as they reached the coal shed, he just jumped and tackled Dale Henderson to the ground. James come tumbling down also while saying,

"Why are you hurting me, I didn't do anything to you."
John then threaten his brother with bodily harm by saying,

"Dale Henderson, if you mention one word about this to our mother, I will hog tie you and wear you out with my belt. Understood?"
He then looked at James and said,

"Did you hear that too?"
James said,
184

"Yes sir, yes sir I did."
John Jr. held Dale on the ground until he promised he would never mention this to anyone.

# C hapter 16

Fall came and went with the whole family putting up the crops. Rebecca was unable to work much in the fields as Gwen was becoming less sufficient as days went by. Mabel's Bryon helped more and more. Each of the children worked very hard to complete the butchering and preparing things for their mother to can, smoke and so on. James George, Edith and Mary Bella had picked all the strawberries and taken care of about everything in the orchard. James would use that little wood wagon his father had made for him to pull the bushel baskets to the house. He was also the one who climbed up into the trees to shake off the ripe fruit. You could hear his warnings to his little sisters as he would scream,

"Geronimo!"

James George, with all of his strength, had also helped so much when making apple butter this year. He stirred and stirred over that big hot copper kettle. His little arms were strong enough to keep going for at least an hour at a time. Out of all the children, James George seemed to be bigger for his age. He was just born with large strong muscles.

All of the younger children seemed to be growing up too fast. John Jr. noticed how they each had become so aware of Gwen's illness. They now often seemed to be completely avoiding the room she was staying in. Were they becoming hardened to death? The poor little things had seen so much of it in their short lives. Or, were they coming to the realization that Gwen was really going to die and they did not know how to deal with that fact.

The doctor had been out to the house several times lately. On one occasion he brought some medicine and gave shots to each and every family member. No one wanted to take the shot, but he called it preventive medicine. He then put a patch on each of their arms and said to leave it there. He said that he would be back to check it in a few days. They learned later that this was to see if anyone else was infected with the tuberculosis. Luckily, no one else in the family showed any signs of the disease. There were no red marks under their patches. This meant they were free of tuberculosis.

By late September, John, Jr. was really feeling the pressures of getting the crops up and the pressures of life in general. Other fellows his age were dating and enjoying life. He would never be able to do any of that kind of stuff. Everett dated, but he had started his dating process long before everything happened around the Dahl house. Besides, John, Jr. was the oldest one left at home and the one who had to take charge. He would often find himself disgusted with Everett when he would take off to see Hazel. Where were his responsibilities? Where were his loyalties? With Hazel he supposed. Oh, he did not begrudge

188

Everett of his romance. Actually he was very happy for him. He just knew he had to bear the whole burden and could not let his guard down for one second. He could not give into life's wishes for himself; not now, not later, maybe not ever. He must be there for his mother and the children.

The school year had started again. The children all rode a bus by now. There was no longer a school at Bunker Hill. Everyone went to Vinton. Some evenings John, Jr. would worry if the bus would be really late. The weather and the dirt roads caused all kinds of problems. He would often wonder at what time he had lost his spot as their carefree and happy oldest brother and became their father figure. Rebecca had tried so hard for him to have a life of his own, but he had just refused. She knew there was a young lady at the church who had her eyes set on John. His mother begged him to call on her. No matter how badly he wanted to do just that, he knew if anything became of it, this pretty young lady would occupy too much of his time. The valuable time he needed to devote to his mother and his siblings. What could he offer this young lady anyway? He could offer her nothing but pain, suffering and hard work? No, she would be better off if she would marry Bill Harden who had just inherited his uncle's big farm. Bill had had his eyes on her for a long time as well. John, Jr. knew he had better quit thinking of such things and keep his priorities straight.

John, Jr. would often have little talks with himself. He would think things like,

"You have several little children and women looking to you for their survival."

He had promised his father he would take care of everyone. This promise was made while his father was on his death bed! His father had that talk with him just days before he died. He had told him exactly what he expected of him. John, Jr. had made the promise that he would take good care of the family. He was determined he would do just that before he would ever seek out a life for himself. After these talks with himself, John, Jr. would often feel like he was being selfish to even have thought such things; especially the thoughts of jealousy over other young men such as his brother having a life. He knew his brother Everett was grieving as well. It was good he had someone like Hazel to help him through all the pain.

One evening in October, Everett, John, Jr. and Dale Henderson were going about their chores when they noticed a calf they had just penned up for butchering next year. This calf was showing some crazy signs. It looked really wild in its eyes and it would not eat. It was decided they would have to keep a close eye on it. Maybe a snake had bitten it or something. They left the barn telling each other they would look its whole body over in the morning, based upon the fact of course, if it was still alive. They would then see if anything had bitten it and so on. It would be lighter in the barn in the morning. They could see very little this late in the evening.

The next morning was once again too dark to see what was wrong with the calf. The children went about their chores. They did notice the calf was lying down and it seemed fairly quiet this morning. The decision was made that someone would come back out to check on it after day light.

By the time Rebecca hit the concrete patio on this particular morning, the only two left in the house asleep were Edith Bea and Mary Bella. Of course Gwen was in the house, but she had already been awake and had been talking with her mother earlier. So the biscuits were surely done by now and the ham she had left on the back burner would be nice and brown. Everything, except the gravy was ready for everyone to eat. As her shoe taps hit that concrete they made a loud clickly-clack sound. This was from that normal run she had instead of a walk. She screamed out in a loud voice,

"Everybody up, you're BURNING SUN-SHINE."

Gwen laughed as she heard that wonderful voice saying those words. She wondered how on earth she ever managed to get up while working in Columbus, Ohio without the presence of her mother screaming out you're Burning Sunshine.

Breakfast went on as usual with everyone quietly passing the food around their large table. James George, who really could not be quiet, had made a remark of how he had an invention. He said,

"When I grow up I will build a table with an extra piece on top of it. That piece would be round like a wheel and you would put all of your food upon it. That way you could just turn it around for everyone to pick what they wanted."

Everyone laughed. John Jr. remarked something about him being a pretty smart young inventor. Rebecca let her mind wonder as she thought of how someday she would like to have some matching chairs. As of right now she had four straight chairs with wicker backs and fronts and

191

two armed chairs matching those. This was a set and they were very pretty. This was a very nice set. These chairs had carved feet that looked like claws. As for the other four chairs they were just mixed and matched tall back chairs. While her mind was wondering over her décor, a sad thought came through. What good was it to worry about matching chairs anymore anyway? Some were empty now due to her losses. With that thought she excused herself from the table and decided to go have her coffee with her daughter, Gwen.

When Rebecca got to Gwen's room she found she had hardly touched her food, but she had a big smile upon her face. She was such a pleasant young lady. She laughed at her mother as she sat down. She was saying,

"I just had a funny thought, mother." Rebecca said,

"And what might that have been young lady?"
She chuckled and said,

"I was just trying to figure out how on earth I ever got up to go to work in Columbus, Ohio without my alarm clock."
Rebecca said,

"Whatever do you mean child?"
Gwen must have been feeling better, because she was being very mischievous at this point. She said,

"Why you, mother! You were not there screaming that I was BURNING SUNSHINE, and I will just have to admit to you that I often did not get up until 6:30 a.m.! Do you believe I will be punished in my afterlife for that?"
Both women laughed and really enjoyed their coffee together. They talked about many things
192

that morning, normal things, not mournful things. As Rebecca left her daughter's room she made a decision that for the rest of Gwen's short life, she was going to be happy and talk about happy things. She could tell that was exactly what her daughter wanted. If she was determined to be so brave and make every minute count so much, then by God she would do the same.

Rebecca walked out of the room and back into the kitchen with a smile on her face. Everyone was finished eating and the girls were gathering up the dishes. The boys were just sitting there sort of staring out into space. There seemed to be a lot of that going around lately. She clapped her hands together as she said,

"Liven up everyone, there is a new rule in this house, Gwen wants us all to live our lives to our fullest. She wants to be happy. She wants all of us to be happy too, so we are going to be happy! **Understood**?"

Everyone laughed. That sounded like music to her ears as she had not heard laugher around there in a long time. Later that morning, this being Saturday, the smaller children were sent to Gwen's room. Since she was feeling better, Rebecca thought this may be good for everyone. They took a puzzle and a large stiff cardboard so they could put it together on Gwen's bed. That should be great fun. John, Jr. told his mother he and the boys were going to go check on that calf. She mentioned she would like to tag along. When they got to the barn, they knew almost immediately what the problem was. Some wild animal had reached through the calf's small pen and obviously bitten him on the leg. This may not have been such a horrible thing had the animal not been

193

rabietic. The calf was foaming at the mouth. Everyone knew he had rabies, an often fatal viral disease that affects the central nervous systems of most warm-blooded animals and is transmitted in the saliva of an infected animal.

Everett was sent to the house to fetch father's shotgun. This animal must be put down. Someone needed to go see the doctor and tell him what had happened at their barn. Everyone understood the seriousness of this situation. There had been a great Uncle George who had been bitten by an infected animal. The family knew that he lived a very short time afterwards. The joy of the morning seemed to slip away really fast. Rebecca knew what was in store for each and every one of the Dahl household.

Once the family arrived back at the house, John, Jr. and Everett washed up and headed for the garage. They were heading towards Dr. Browns'. They knew he would not expect the whole family to come to his office with Gwen's condition, so they must go convince him to put them on his visiting schedule just as soon as possible.

As they walked into the office, the doctor was coming from his examining room. He laid some papers upon his daughter's desk. She worked as his secretary and receptionist. Before she could say good-morning, Doc Brown said,

"Top-of-morning to you two Mr. Dahl's, how are you boys this morning."

They proceeded to tell him of their dilemma. Everett could not help but remark to John of how that doctor is always so calm about everything. The good doctor asked them what they had done with the animal. They informed him they had killed it and were going to bury it when they returned home. Doc Brown said,

"Oh, no boys, you are going to need to burn that animal. Get you some wood, make a pile and throw the calf on the top of that stack and burn it." They agreed to do just that and then ask what to do about those exposed to this rabietic disease. The doctor told them to just sit down a minute while he finished up with the patient he had in the examining room and he would be free to talk with them. The handsome young men found a seat and sat down. They could not help but notice the young lady behind the desk would look at each of them, then quickly look away. It was quite obvious she found the rugged farm boys attractive. This went straight over John's head, but Everett had thoughts of fixing his big brother up with the doctor's daughter. He walked over to her desk, wearing a big smile and said,

"Good-morning Irene! How are you this bright and shinning morning?"
She said,

"I'm fine! How are you?"
She smiled up at him and asked him if he would like a book or catalog to look at. He replied that he did not, but he told her that maybe his big brother John would like one. John now realizing what his crazy brother was up to, said in a harsh like voice,

"No thank you! I'm just fine!"
When Everett was trying to get his long legs back into the seat away from the table in front of it, John punched him in the side and said,

"Behave!"

Dr. Brown walked out with Mrs. Davenport. She was a friendly lady who lived down the street from his office. She had lost her husband a few years ago and now spent much of her time writing a little gossip column for the local newspaper. John, Jr. and Everett both felt their muscles tightening up. All they needed now was for her to get wind of their predicament and the whole world would know. They heard the doctor tell her to quit staying up so late of nights and to just drink some warm milk before she went to bed, and that he was sure she would feel better in no time at all. She stopped at Irene's desk to tell her how pretty she believed she looked today. Then she noticed the Dahl boys. John, Jr. thought of how their family must be a wonderful source for her news column, as she had written so much about their trials and tribulations in the past few years. Now, that stupid cow would probably give her still more to write about. He could just see the headlines: 'The tragedies of the Dahl's'! They could tell by the look in her eyes, she was sure she was going to get some news today. Mrs. Davenport said,

"Good-morning gentlemen, please don't tell me Gwen has worsened."

"No,"

Everett answered very quickly,

"She just ran out of some of her medicine." John thought of how his brother should not have lied, but was somewhat relieved that he did. She seemed to accept that little white lie with a smile and told them to tell their mother and everyone else that she said hello. She then walked out of the door.

The doctor motioned for the young men to go into his office. He said,

196

"I hate to be the bad guy here, but you know you all have to take shots to prevent this virus from attacking your bodies."
Both boys knotted up and said,
"Yes sir!"
He told them to pull up their shirts; he would just start them on their shots right away. Everett felt tears form in his eyes as the doctor put a long needle into his stomach. Lord that was painful. He stood there and watched as his brother received the same shot. Dr. Brown told the boys he must get out to the house as soon as possible because every member of the family had to have these same shots. Gwen was the only one who had not been to the barn. That meant the little children and mother must all take these dreaded shots as well.

John, Jr. went out to drive home. As he got into the car, he hit his fist upon the steering wheel and he replied in a loud voice,

"What else can happen? Everett, you tell me just what else can happen to us?"

The rest of the three miles to the farm house was quiet. Neither boy said a thing. When they got into the house, both started talking at the very same time while telling their mother what had to be done. This may have been rude, but coming from this large family they were often somehow able to listen and talk at the same time. Mother seemed to take it quite well. She already knew what the outcome was going to be. She asked when the doctor was coming and they told her no later than tomorrow afternoon. They then ask her if she knew this was a series of shots and if she knew they were very painful. She just replied with a remark like,

"We'll pray for comfort and we'll just have to do what we have to do."

Times like this, their mother sometimes looked like an old wash cloth someone had just rung out one too many times and there was not a drop of water left in it. Their hearts went out to her.

The two older sons told Dale Henderson, they needed his help. Of course James George wanted to come along. He felt he would be needed as well, but this is one job they preferred he not be included in. They teamed up the horses, got a wagon, got a stack of wood and went to the barn. They got the calf and dragged it upon the wagon. They then hauled everything out into the big pasture and built a fire. They stayed there about an hour waiting for it all to burn away. They sat on the side of the fire where the wind was not blowing in their direction. It still made them feel dirty, so they sat there discussing of how they could not wait to get back to the house to take a bath. Dale Henderson remarked,

"Hey, it's not even Saturday night."
They laughed and remembered what mother had said about how we were all going to be happy and to count our blessings every day. Someone came up with,

"Well, guess we had a blessing. That thing did not bite us."
Their moods were changing and by the time they returned to the house they were all joking and laughing about one thing or another.

As they threw open the door to the kitchen, laughing and in good spirits, Rebecca said,

198

"I did not know it would be so much fun to burn a cow, or I would have suggested burning one much earlier."

They just laughed again and this time Rebecca laughed with them. Gwen hollered from the bedroom,

"What's so funny?"

They all went to her door and said we will tell you all about it just as soon as we have had baths. She in turn said,

"Hey you guys, it is not Saturday night." Now the whole family was laughing and joyful. Yes they did have blessings. Many of them! Rebecca thought of how now if everyone can just remember that and be thankful for their beautiful family.

# C hapter 17

John, Jr. and the others made sure Christmas was nice again that year for everyone. Aunt Beatrice and Uncle Robert had brought their group down for three whole days. This is the first time anyone had laughed so much or enjoyed anything this much since last March. They had a wonderful Christmas. Everyone went along to get a tree. Mother and Aunt Bea cooked and baked. Gwen was able to set up throughout the holidays and everyone felt it did her a world of good to see he beloved cousin Alice. You could hear nothing but giggles coming from that bedroom. Sometime by this date, some doctors had come up with the idea of how workers needed protection. Too late for Gwen, but Beatrice and her family had long since been given the preventative medicine due to their work at the hospital. Thankfully this opened the way so everyone felt safe in coming to visit.

As soon as Christmas was over, the family celebrated James George's birthday. Rebecca hated it being so close to Christmas. She felt he did not get the honors he so deserved. He was such a loving child. She often contributed that to the fact his birthday was so very close to the date of our Savior's birth. The young lad did not seem to mind that his birthday cake was often just a half of a cake. This cake was usually a cake that had been left over from Christmas. He also did not seem to mind that he had to save one of his gifts from Christmas for his birthday. It had become a little game to him when he decided which one it should be. Thank God, this Christmas had caused Rebecca to be more thankful for what she had instead of what she did not have. She thanked God for all her blessings. She thanked Him for causing Gwen to be better and for having such a wonderful, enjoyable holiday season.

All good things have to come to an end. Everyone went home and the house seemed sort of empty. The shots everyone had to take were long over by now, but Doctor Brown had stopped by a few days after Christmas to check on Gwen. He said that the visit from the family members had done her a world of good. She was cheerful with the doctor. As Rebecca walked him to the door, he stopped and said,

"Just a minute! My wife sent you some cookies. I will need to go to the car to get them." Rebecca said she would just follow him to the car. As the doctor reached into the car he said,

"Rebecca, you do know she is not any better, don't you? This *is* terminal!"
Rebecca said,

"Why do you have to remind me?"
He leaned his tall structure over to where his eyes met hers and said,

"I just don't want anyone to get any false hopes. She is going to have good days and she is going to have bad days. That young lady is going to do her very best not to let you know of the bad days. She loves you all so much and feels badly that her illness is hurting the whole family. She has made peace with her death and said she is ready to go. She said she is even getting excited now about seeing John. I told her to be sure to tell him I said hello and that I miss my dear old friend."

Rebecca started to cry at this time. The good doctor said,

"I did not want to make you cry Rebecca. Dying is such a part of living and we all must do that sooner or later. We do not understand why someone as young and as beautiful as your sweet daughter has to go, but we don't want her to suffer either, now do we?"

She knew this all to be so true. She said her goodbyes to the doctor and thanked him for everything. She hollered back at him as he started the car asking him to please thank Myrtle for the cookies. As Rebecca went back into the house, the bedroom in which Gwen was staying drawled her like a magnet. She looked in only to find her beautiful daughter sound asleep. The doctor must have given her something to make her rest. The mother just stood there adoring her pretty frail child. She was darker than any of the other children. She had taken more after Rebecca's side of the family and did not have that robust, larger than life, healthy and strengthening looks that so many of the Dahl's had. All the rest of John and Rebecca's children had that robust look except Gwen and Dale Henderson. The Dahl's were of a bigger bone or something. She just couldn't put her finger on it. Right now she wondered if Gwen had been something besides so tiny maybe she could live longer.

203

All of Rebecca's children were beautiful, but Gwen was like a frail paper flower or a dainty little angel. Her black hair shined in the light and it looked just like a dark blue glass. She wondered how it could shine after all of the medicine they continually had to put into her frail little body. As she continued to stare at her daughter knowing in her heart she would not always be able to see her. She thought of how a farm girl she was not meant to be, no matter how good she was at it. She just did not have the frame. God must have sent her here to make us all happy and now he needs her back in heaven to write His poetry.

Every spare minute Gwen ever had was spent listening to the Victrola or writing poetry. She had written some really beautiful poems. Before this illness, Rebecca had always wished for her pretty daughter to meet her prince and pictured the little petite girl in fancy gowns, dancing with the one she loved. She could see her floating across the floor with her face all aglow. Now this was never going to happen for her daughter. She couldn't help but wonder if there was not some beau left alone in Columbus, Ohio, sitting there wondering what had happened to his beautiful princess. Rebecca knew in her heart she was not going to ever ask that question. If Gwen wanted her to know she would have told her. Besides, Gwen had written many letters to her friends in the city and she was sure Alice would have informed every one of her fate.

Rebecca kept up her good cheer for her family all through the New Year. They had sort of a party-dinner on the New Year's Eve. They set up a table in Gwen's room and the whole family joined in with singing and playing games. Gwen

204

looked so frail by now. It was all she could do to keep her little head on the pillow. But she kept a beautiful smile upon her face as the old year went out and the New Year came in.

Valentine's week, Gwen had worked all week long giving poems to each of the children to put on their homemade cards. She was no longer able to sit up long enough to write them down herself, but Mabel had become her hands and she had been writing all of her letters and poems for her for the past month. This week was no different. Mabel would write each poem down for each child to copy, as Gwen would think of a verse. The children would then take them upstairs and write them in their own hand writing and put them in their own form upon their cards. As thanks and to show their love to Gwen, the other children had all secretly made a very large card while upstairs. They decorated it and every member of the family had signed it. Even mother signed it. They then waited until Valentine's Day and gave it to Gwen. She cried, but wanted to assure her loving family immediately that the tears were tears of joy.

By Easter Gwen was so weak she could no longer sit up at all. Mabel and her mother were feeding her by sticking a spoon into her mouth and praying she would swallow at least some of it. They also prayed that they would not choke her in the process. There was so much strength and love inside that little piece of flesh and bones lying upon that bed. She would always smile. She would even whisper when her voice was about gone. She would whisper that she was so sorry to be a burden to anyone. Rebecca and the others could not imagine where she could get that kind of strength. She surely must be an angel!

Gwen had better days to where someone could sit and read to her. One day Mabel dragged out all of her hope chest items and showed each and every one of them to Gwen. Gwen smiled at each item and said in a weak voice,

"That's nice."

Or

"That's pretty."

As all the items had been shown and Mabel was ready to leave the room, Gwen called her back into the room to say,

"I like your Bryon. Please be happy for me and tell your children I would have loved to have met them. Maybe God will let me have just a peek when they are born. Do you suppose?"

Mabel turned her back and could barely get away from the door before she broke down completely. She cried the biggest part of that night. Rebecca went to comfort her, but knew she couldn't comfort anyone. The fact was,

"Gwen was going to die."

Gwen's Aunt Ethel had crocheted a bed jacket for her and wanted to give it to her for her birthday. Her birthday was going to be May 18th. On the 10th day of May, Ethel came down to the house and told Rebecca,

"I don't know why, but I want to give Gwen her present now. I just can't wait to see her eyes when she sees it. I think I did a pretty good job on it, if I do say so myself."

They opened the box to see a pretty ivory colored bed jacket. Rebecca took one look at it and said it was beautiful and of how she was sure Gwen would love it. Both ladies walked into Gwen's room. Rebecca said,

"Gwen, wake up darling. Your Aunt Ethel has a birthday gift for you. She thought you deserved it early because of your good behavior." Gwen smiled and sort of chuckled as she said,

"You shouldn't have, but you know me I love gifts."
Ethel took the bed jacket from the box and Rebecca raised Gwen up so the two women could put the jacket on her frail body. She gazed lovingly up to each woman and said,

"You two are just too much. Aunt Ethel, this is beautiful."
She then asked,

"Aunt Ethel, why did you spend so much time making me such a lovely gift?"
Ethel just said,

"Because I love you child!"
They told her they did not want to tire her and both ladies walked slowly out of the room feeling the weight of knowing her days were numbered. They went out into the parlor and both just let the tears roll down their faces. They could hear Gwen saying something in her weak little voice, so they stepped closer to the door. Gwen said,

"Alright, I know you two are crying, even though you are trying not to let me know."
Ethel mustered up enough voice to say,

"What makes you think that darling?"
Gwen just said,

"Because neither of you can be quiet that long."
They walked back to her door and heard her say,

"Please don't cry for me. I have had a wonderful life even if it has been a short one.

Maybe God doesn't plan for everyone to have a lot of years. Maybe I have completed what He wanted me to do on this planet. Yes, I am going to leave you soon, but I am going to a better place and I am going to be with father. Is there anything you two would like for me to tell him?"

They tried to smile and both said at the same time to tell him that they loved him. Gwen went on with her lecture,

"Please have faith in God. He has a plan. We may not understand that plan, but He does have a plan."

They listened very carefully to what she had to say and then each went back into the room and kissed her on the forehead. They told her how much they loved her. As the ladies left the room once more; Rebecca wondered where on earth this brave young girl got so much strength. It seemed to come from somewhere deep within. Should it be her turn to go, she does not believe she could face it with so much bravery.

Everyone tried to go to church as much as they could. The weather was getting better but the roads were terribly wet. One of the older children would drive, if they could, and make sure everyone was in Sunday school. Rebecca got to go only occasionally anymore. The only time she could go was when Mabel would trade off times with her or Ethel would just insist that Rebecca go and she would stay with Gwen.

As time came closer for Gwen's birthday, Rebecca and the others started planning some sort of a birthday party. She was going to be twenty-one and that called for a celebration. Everyone knew she was too weak for much, but they were going to do something. This plan became a little game. Gwen would ask what was going on as she could feel there was some sort of a secret. Mr. Swick had come by with his traveling store. Different members of the family had purchased what little they could for a gift for Gwen. Others were busy hand making gifts for her. Rebecca had gotten her a silver brush set a while back and was waiting until her birthday to give it to her.

On the sixteenth of May, Gwen had a passing out spell and they had brought Dr. Brown back to check on her. He said it was just the terminal reactions of her illness and nothing could be done except to make her as comfortable as possible. He also warned that it would not be long now. After that spell, the older children decided she was coming and going too much and they wanted to make her happy, so they convinced their mother to just go ahead and bake a cake and they would have an early birthday party.

The good Lord must have been in that decision, because on May the 17th, 1933 Gwen Rebecca Dahl passed away. Just one day before her twenty first birthday. She died while still at the age of twenty. She went to sleep never to awaken again. She just closed her beautiful eyes and silently went to another place. Rebecca nearly died away herself. Losing yet another of her precious loved ones. Now it was her beautiful, beautiful daughter. She knew Gwen had suffered so and she could not expect her to want to stay around any longer. Even breathing had been so hard for her to do, and she needed the relief. She was hanging on as long as she could to spare the pain to her family. Everyone knew they had to let her go.

Once again each member of the family handled their grief in their own ways. John, Jr. went to a corner of the barn and had his crying hours. Mabel cried on Bryon's shoulder, Everett brought Hazel home to stay the few days and depended on her for support. Dale Henderson would hardly let John, Jr. out of his site. Other times he would just go trim trees. That seemed to be an outlet for him. The younger children had often called him Johnny Apple-seed; making light of the way he tended to the fruit trees. James George and the girls just clung together and at mothers skirt tales. Once the rest of the family came in, food came from everywhere again. This ever getting smaller family clung to each other and went through the motions of yet another funeral.

The sun was shining on the day they put Gwen into the ground. It was a beautiful day just as she would have wanted. The church was full again. Robert and Beatrice had brought along some of Gwen's city friends. You could see the hurt upon their faces at the thoughts of losing their friend at such a young age. Once again the minister said,

"God givith and God takith away."
Rebecca could only feel the takith away part now. She had known this death was coming for months but that did not make it any easier to accept. At this point she did not care if anyone saw her cry. She did not care if anyone liked or disliked her old dark green velvet dress and hat. She did not even care if it was acceptable or not. She hated it by now, as it was officially her funeral dress. Each time she wore it, she had just lost a very big piece of her very being.

210

She stood for a long time by the grave site talking to her deceased husband John and telling him Gwen's care was now in God's and his hands. She got on her knees by the casket and let it all go and cried her heart out. No one, including John, Jr., attempted to make her leave. He even got down there with her and cried as his big heart was breaking as well. She looked around only to find each and every one of her children on their knees upon that green cloth rug like thing. They were all crying like their hearts would surely break. Each had their arms upon the other's shoulders. It was as if to say to the world,

"I'm sorry but we're hurting and we don't really want to try to hide it any longer."
They could hear people praying for this poor family. They could hear people crying all the way down the path as they were trying to leave. Doctor Brown had insisted the family needed to be left alone after about an hour. So one by one the funeral attendees were leaving the grave site. Beatrice and Ethel walked up close together as they told Rebecca and the children that they, along with Chancy would be waiting at the cars when they were ready to go. They said for Rebecca and her children to stay right where they were for just as long as they wanted to.

Rebecca did not know how long they had stayed upon their knees at that grave site. She just knew there was no one left there but them and the cars with their ever-so-patient waiting family members. She saw Mr. Wise with two of his sons sitting upon a wagon close by. She knew they were hired to close the grave. He spoke as they passed and you could see he had so much pity in his eyes. His boys had been crying and they did not even know Gwen. It must have been some site watching a whole family upon a ground crying and clinging together. Everyone knew this family was just devastated with yet another death. This day, the whole countryside's hearts bled for the Dahl family.

From that day through the summer months everyone just went through the motions. They did not say much. The littlest children did not even play. Bella was the only one who did not act as though she understood everything. She would get cheerful once in a while only to be quieted by one of the older children. One night Edith came into Rebecca's room and asked,

"Mommy am I going to die?"
Rebecca answered by saying,

"Yes, someday angel. Why do you ask?"
She had overheard some of the older children saying they wondered who would be next. This conversation must have taken place on one of their down feeling days. One of them had stressed how the black cloud over their household was just waiting to take another loved one. Rebecca told her that was silly and she was just a little girl. That Gwen had passed away for two reasons. One was that Daddy wanted her to come to be with him and another was that God considered her an angel and He needed her back in Heaven. He missed having her write His poems. She was only supposed to be on earth for a short time. This seemed to please the little round faced girl and she ran off to play with her dolls.

This conversation was also another turning point in Rebecca's life. She remembered the joy Gwen's life had given her. The joy it had given all of them and she had a long talk with the children
212

to get them to remember how Gwen did not want them to grieve over her. She told of how she wanted them to celebrate her life. They started setting up a time for each person to read one of Gwen's poems. She had a large book of them and reading one every night was going to keep her close to them. Thus, the healing process had begun.

By fall everyone was accepting the death more readily. They were making more trips to Elizabeth's while watching Simon grow. Everett and Hazel were spending as much time together as they could. John, Jr. and Dale Henderson were helping Everett work on that old log cabin. It was coming around. Rebecca had ridden with the boys on the old buckboard one day while they were on one of their lumber trips. She liked what she saw so far and was very proud of her boys for doing such a good job. She was sure Hazel would be pleased. It was a far cry from the home John had brought her home to that evening so many years ago.

Chancy and Majel seemed to be able to come by more often lately, which was wonderful. Ethel and her family came often too. Uncle Andy had invited everyone down to dinner one night and they had gone. They enjoyed that very much. The children loved that big old house. They had a very unusual piano. They called it a player piano. Someone would pump it like an organ and it would play songs. It was funny to watch the keys go up and down with no one playing it. Andy's children had a bad habit of sliding down the winding stair case. Rebecca remembered that from her childhood and knew how very dangerous it was to attempt such a ride. She also knew how

213

great fun it was. So she wasn't too upset when she learned her little ones had ridden down the rails. This was while she and her sister-in-law were in the kitchen and Andy and the older children were outside. She just felt lucky no one was hurt.

One week Elizabeth and Simon came and spent the whole week with the family. This was a good time for everyone. After John, Jr. would get done with his chores; he would many times go somewhere in the Model T. Rebecca never questioned him because she knew in her heart he was going to visit Gwen and his father. Sometimes he would take things to cut the grass. Other times she knew he just wanted some quiet time with the loved ones who had gone and left them. Some Sunday's after church the whole family would go and get on their knees and have prayer over the graves. They almost always said a speech that seemed like in unison upon their departure,

"We love you father and we love you Gwen."

The family coped as best they could. They knew their lives had to go on.

# Chapter 18

By late September 1933 John Dahl, Jr. was feeling the pressures of getting the crops in and the pressures of trying to help raise his siblings. He worried all of the time. He tried so hard to do everything right, but in reality he had just turned twenty-four years old on July eleventh and was too young to have such responsibilities. Thank God, mother had seemed to be more cheerful and was facing life once again. She was a very strong woman by now and he knew she would soon be able to keep everything going. He just hated to have her work so hard, so he tried to take as much of the burden from her as possible.

John, Jr. was a tall thin man. He looked very much like his father. He had darker hair than his father, but his facial features were very much the same. He had high cheek bones and sharp bone features. He was very handsome in his own right. Pauline, from the church was still very interested in him. He finally took her to a church social. Rebecca was so happy he finally gave into all the pressures everyone had put upon him to do just that. He had felt he had nothing to offer her and cared enough for her to hope she would start liking another guy at the church. He felt this person would be so much better for her. However, she had stayed true to her desire. She had wanted to be with John and finally he had asked her out.

Homecoming at church was a wonderful day for Rebecca and the children. Everyone was home for the occasion. Elizabeth, Simon and her husband Matthew were all there for the week-end. It was great to see all of the people who had moved away. Rebecca was happy everyone was able to come home for the gathering. The Wyman's children were all home as well. Rebecca could not help but feel pride boost up inside of her when she looked over to under the oak tree and saw so many young people on quilts. They were all laughing and talking with each other. There was John, Jr. and Pauline, Everett and Hazel, Mabel and Bryon, Elizabeth and Matthew and several other young couples. She smiled as she thought of how most of the couples were hers. Simon was running around very close under grandma's feet. It was so good to see the beautiful young people enjoying this pretty fall day. Everyone in the community seemed to be very good cooks. So, the food was also wonderful.

Rebecca had to laugh when she looked over and saw that James was standing upon a couple of blocks preaching to a group of children. Edith Bea and Mary Bella were sitting on the ground with both legs crossed as if they were listening to him for the very first time. They must really enjoy his goings on. She just smiled and walked on past them. A few weeks ago, Uncle Andy had had an auction to sell some of his stock. Rebecca had taken the children down to play while she helped her sister-in-law prepare food for the large crowd. James had sat right up front with his uncle and seemed spellbound by the whole affair. Now she worried her loud little son might break out into being an auctioneer at any minute. He had been mixing a lot of preaching and a lot of auctioneering lately and that would not be appropriate for church. It was almost time for services to begin, so maybe she was safe. She was very excited about the upcoming service because there were to be several good singing groups there today.

After the homecoming, the month seemed to fly by. There was so much to do before cold weather set in. In October, Rebecca started working on Christmas gifts. John, Jr. and Everett started the same thing. John and Everett had taken shop in school and had also watched their father build toys enough to where they were getting pretty good at these projects themselves. They had been working so hard on that old cabin. She would guess they were getting to be pretty good at carpentry as well.

During the winter, several of the local farm ladies got together for quilting bees. This was much fun and they turned out some beautiful quilts. Rebecca was determined to have a nice quilt done for Everett and Hazel before their wedding. It was scheduled on September first of the next year. She was working on a wedding ring style quilt. She would never have had time to do this in the spring and summer. So much of her winter was spent making Christmas gifts until Christmas, then sewing on this quilt.

217

During the winters it was hard to get a lot done at night. It got dark so early. Everything had to be done by the oil lamps. The farm was so demanding. Everyone had to be up by about five thirty each morning so they were ready for bed no later than nine-thirty at night. Thank God for the bigger children. They spent their evenings with homework of their own and then helped the younger children get theirs. Edith seemed to love geography. No matter how many times Rebecca would ask her not to write in her book because Mary Bella would need it too. She would still do it. She wrote all over the South American pictures telling of how she wished to go there someday. She had drawn a picture of herself standing at the top of the mountain that looked like a loaf of bread. Oh well, she was sure Mary Bella would not mind any of this very much because she was Edith's shadow anyway. She could never see any wrong her bigger sister might do.

Books were expensive and Rebecca was determined to not buy one more. All of their books had lasted through all of the children to this point and they would just have to make do with them a few more years. Each year Rebecca had made new jackets for the books. This kept them pretty clean. Rumors were, some of the city schools were now being funded by the government to where parents did not have to buy the children's books. Rebecca couldn't help but wish this had happened years before and aided with the purchase for her children.

The winter of 1933 and 1934 was a cold one indeed. Christmas came and went with not much fan fair. Rebecca was thankful both the girls and James George were doing well in school this year. She had worried so much about their grades since they had been kept out of school so much in the fall. This was not that unusual in farm country. All of the local farmers had to keep at least their sons out during harvest season. All the young men had to work in the crops. The Dahl's had been lucky by having the older boys who helped John, Sr. to get their crops up. They had never had to keep the little younger ones out before.

Work was getting harder for John, Jr. He wondered if it was the weather being so cold or because he had been so sick at his stomach lately. He was feeling the pressures of trying to do the things he thought his father would have done. Tragedy sometimes makes a family closer and stronger, but they still had their little disagreements sometimes. Just last week John, Jr. had gotten into it with Mabel. She had left a romance magazine laying on the wagon where all the children could have seen it. Not that there was anything wrong with the book, John just felt with their religion his parents would not have approved. In her defense she stated that Elizabeth had given it to her. This made him upset with Elizabeth, thinking of how she was even older and should have known better. It was just something he felt was for older children and in his eyes Mabel was still a child. Mabel had jerked it out of his hand and told him it was nothing to him.

Mabel did not like John Jr. trying to be like a father figure to her and she told him so much. She said,

"You're not my father! You will never be my father! And, just in case you didn't know it, my father died! Remember?"

219

He snapped right back at her and said,

"Grow up Mabel! You are supposed to be the oldest girl in this family now with Elizabeth and Gwen gone!"

He went on in a loud mad voice to say,

"We have a crisis here, in case you haven't noticed! I will talk to you later about the mending of your ways!"

With that he stomped off while very mad at her. Of course this also caused her to stomp off and refuse to work with him the rest of that day. As John dragged his tired body in through the door that evening, Mabel met him at that door, hugged him and said she was sorry. That is the way this family handled any disagreement. They just hugged and made up. Other than a few little quarrels such as this, the family got along very well.

It had been planned for Mabel to go to nursing school and being placed at Saint Mary's Hospital in Huntington, West Virginia. This city was just across the Ohio River. It was about sixty miles down the road. John, Jr. liked Bryon Wyman very well, but felt the couple was getting just a little too close. She was eighteen now and out of high school. For some reason, it seemed as if no one even talked about a higher education for her anymore. Instead she often spoke of how it would be when she and Bryon got married. Although nothing had ever been stated officially about that either. John, Jr. decided he would rake his brain on how he could someway afford for her to complete her education. When in these thoughts he would often just hang his head in regret. He knew the crops had not been all that good lately so he had no idea how he could accomplish these tasks. He would get frustrated with his mother on occasion too, because she now felt there was absolutely no way any of the younger children could ever go on for a higher education. She seemed determined to resolve herself to that thought. He was just as determined they were going to get that education! Someway, somehow!

One day in January John, Jr. was working in the barn with his brothers. He got really sick and went outside to relieve everything in his stomach. Dale Henderson wanted to run and tell mother still again, but John, Jr. would not allow him. He said it was just something he had eaten and he would be alright after a while. He knew he most drink some milk or something as these pains seemed more frequent lately. So he went to the house and drank some milk and felt better almost instantly.

January was unreasonably cold this year. John, Jr. was increasingly feeling the pressure of the responsibility of trying to keep a family together. Mother was becoming a stronger woman, not to say she had not always been strong, but she could work just as long and just as hard as anyone else; usually harder. She sometimes had such a lost, haunting look in her eyes, but John, Jr. never caught her crying again. He knew she was using every effort to keep her best face on for the children.

Neighbors were wonderful. During the thirties times were rough on everyone, but their relatives and their neighbors never ceased to offer a helping hand. The whole community was God loving people whose hearts went out to the Dahl family. You know the farmers around there were

221

just as exhausted and tired as anyone else after they had completed their chores. But after their chores, they would often come over themselves or send one of their eldest sons to see if they could help the Dahl's. This was really good of everyone. However, John, Jr. would just about as soon the Wyman's would keep Bryon at home a little more. John was probably just being over protective, but he felt Bryon had way too much interest in Mabel. Besides, his interest in Mabel kept him from being of much help to anyone anyway. Becoming more of a father figure, John was in no hurry to give his sister to this young man just yet. Not for him to keep anyway!

John's stomach problems became worse as the days past. He would double over completely with pain from time to time. New Years, he had planned a party for the children and was going to invite some neighboring children along with cousins and so on. He thought maybe this would bring some normalcy into this house of sadness. He worked with mother to decorate and plan for this party. They would watch the New Year in and everyone visiting would spend the night to sing and just have fun. John, Jr. was looking so forward to this himself. The girls made paper ropes and hung them from one corner of the room to the other. Mabel had made and glued little pointed hats together and Dale and James had made some noise makers. It was going to be great fun.

The party was a big hit! Everyone had a good time. Rebecca sang and laughed with the teens and little children. It was crazy at this time of the year, but they dragged out the old ice-cream maker and even made ice cream. This went swell with the sweet chocolate cake mother had baked. Their Aunt Ethel helped too. She had brought deviled eggs and lots of sandwiches. After the evening settled down and most had gone to bed, John felt very nauseated and went to the barn so no one would see him. He sure did not want to worry anyone. As of late, food and he just weren't getting along too well. This time it scared him, as he vomited up blood.

"Dear God, what is wrong with me,"
he thought.

"I know those apples I ate must have been too tart, but that should not have caused this."

Three days later just as John, Jr. was tossing a fork of hay to the cattle, he became nauseated again. Once again he vomited up blood. Dale Henderson was present. This time John could not catch the little buzzard as he ran to tell mother. He mustered up enough strength to head towards the house. He was not feeling very well, but now had very little pain. Once he got to the house, he laughed it all off because he could see the worry on his mother's face. He told her about the apples and that seemed to satisfy her for the moment; even though she raised an eye brow and he could still see concern deep down in her eyes.

The rest of January John, Jr. seemed to freeze a little more than usual. He knew he had lost some weight and wondered what could have caused all of that. It was a very cold winter and he was having some kind of stomach problems to where he wasn't very hungry most of the time. He would laugh at those thoughts and think of how one should weigh a lot more during winter months so the fat could keep them warm.

# C hapter 19

Dale Henderson opened the barn door on the evening of February the 12th, 1934 to see his brother John, Jr. sitting in front of a puddle of what looked like nothing but blood. John, Jr. was white as a ghost. Unlike all the arguments before, this time Dale got no argument from his brother when he stated he was going to go get mother.

Rebecca ran all the way to the barn to find her eldest son doubled over in pain. Two farms down the road, one of their neighbors had gotten one of those new phone boxes. This was something the Dahl's knew they could not afford. Rebecca had felt it was just a wasteful luxury. Today, she was so thankful the neighbors had splurged on such a box. She immediately sent Dale Henderson on a run to call an ambulance. Things were changing around the farm country. The funeral home in Vinton had recently purchased an ambulance. Thank God for progress. The ambulance would get her son to Doc Brown's faster than she could get someone else to take him.

Her son Everett was off with the Model T somewhere. This seemed to be the very best solution. Thankfully, Vinton was only three miles down the road.

The ambulance arrived in about twenty minutes, but it seemed like hours to Rebecca. All she could do in the meantime was put damp clothes upon John, Jr.'s head, pray, kiss him and tell him she loved him. She had screamed for help and the other children were busy running back and forth to the house bringing more towels, lots of water and glasses of milk. Rebecca just kept repeating to her son of how life had been just too rough for him and that she knew he had the weight of the world upon his shoulders. She kept telling him he was going to be okay and he would get well. She would tell him of how she was going to do something about taking some of these big burdens away from him. She kept saying,

"You have a virus. It will go away."
She'd say,

"God loves us and God is looking out for us."
John, Jr. looked up at his mother and he knew at this minute, she did not believe he would get well, nor did she believe anything she was saying. Behind that tough exterior he saw pure terror, pure unadulterated fear.

When the ambulance arrived, Rebecca was so relieved to see Dr. Brown in the front seat beside of Mr. Coy. One look at John, Jr. and Doc Brown said,

"Rebecca, we are going to take him on to Gallipolis to the hospital. Do you want to ride along?"

226

She told the other children to send someone up to Ethel's or over to the Wyman's and ask if one of the ladies would come to help Mabel. She told Mabel to stay with the children. They agreed, and off went the ambulance with John, Jr. and his mother. The car was moving as fast as Mr. Coy could drive it over the rutted dirt roads.

Once they arrived at the hospital, John, Jr. was rushed into the emergency room. Upon an examination, the doctors decided he had ruptured ulcers. They said they had been ruptured for several days. They felt that now, only time would tell if poisons had gone all through his body. If left unattended a rupture of such things can lead to the poisons getting out into the blood stream and this becomes very serious. As Dr. Brown stood there holding her trembling hands, he stressed to Rebecca that John, Jr. should have told someone earlier of his pains. He said that waiting as long as he had to get treatment could be devastating. Rebecca knew John, Jr. had kept this all a big secret. She knew he did that because of all the pain she had been through. He did not want to worry her. This made her feel very guilty for not noticing what was going on.

Once again, Rebecca found herself walking the floors in that numb state of mind, praying and praying. Saying in her now weaken voice,

"Dear God, not another child! Have I done anything to displease You? Please heal my son!"

All sorts of doubts entered her mind. Maybe she did not pray enough. Maybe if she had been as faithful to her religion as she should have been, this cup would pass from her. Maybe she was too vain. Like the times she would drag out her old clothes and dress up with the big hats, just

227

to make herself feel better or to just know she was still alive. No, a brief thought passed over her as she knew she mainly did that to entertain the little ones. She would dress them up as well. Had she sinned? She kept searching her soul for the reason why one family could have so much stress. So much loss. She then told herself that it all boiled down to God's will. He always knows best, but it is so hard for humans to understand in cases like this. John Jr. just had to get better; God surely would not take another one of her family. Not now in such a short time. He was not a cruel God.

All night Rebecca prayed for the healing power from above. She ask forgiveness of anything she may have done to displease God. She cried and prayed all night long. The next morning she had finally fallen asleep in a chair near her son's bed. A noise awakened her. She looked over to her beloved son. He was so pale. He was sort of a yellow like color. A nurse was taking his temperature. The nurse looked over and smiled at Rebecca. She said,

"Good morning! You must be Mr. John's mother. My name is Phyllis and I will be looking after your son today."

She then reached down to change some bandages where the doctor had placed some sort of a tube. Rebecca smiled back at the nurse and told her if she needed any help to let her know. Rebecca explained that she too was a nurse once upon a time. However, having the nursing training that she had was not helping her way of thinking much this morning. Instead, it caused her much pain because she knew by looking at the patient through nurse's eyes that the prognoses would not be good. She could tell her son's color was all

228

wrong. His temperature was not good and the chance of him surviving was about fifty, fifty. She knew that is exactly what she would have told a parent at this time, should it have been left up to her and someone like John would have been her patient.

That day started out as a very tense one. Rebecca could see the rays of sun shining through the closed drapes of the hospital room. Dr. Brown was going to come by a little later. John, Jr. would go in and out of consciences. His temperature would rise and fall. Every once in a while he would wake up and look at his mother and smile. He would say something like,

"Everything is going to be alright mother. Please don't worry."
Then late in the afternoon while his temperature was high, John, Jr. woke up just a few seconds and looked at his mother to tell her he had just seen Gwen and his father walking along a beautiful river. He added it was even prettier than the Ohio. He said they were walking hand in hand and Gwen had said to come on and join them. She had told him that he would love it there.

Rebecca hid her tears as she realized her son was not going to make it. She knew he had just seen Heaven. She held him in her arms and told him how much she loved him. He then just went to sleep, never to wake up any more. Maybe one would say it was just time for John, Jr. to go but Rebecca could not understand why. Why her son, at his young age. Why would God take him away from her? After losing Gwen, the other children would surely be devastated by the news of losing still another family member?

Rebecca knew John, Jr. had gone on when she heard the last breath leave her son's body. This did not keep her from passing out when a doctor; one she did not know, said John Jr. had died at such and such a time. She woke up to find herself in a wheelchair with someone handing her a pill and a glass of water. She refused the pill but drank the water. She noticed she could not move. Finally Dr. Brown showed up. He told the nurse to leave her in the wheelchair and that he would bring it back to the hospital. He told them he would be taking Mrs. Dahl home. He pushed her out through the parking lot with neither person saying one word. He picked her frail little body up and sat her in the front seat of his car. He folded the chair and placed it in the back seat. He climbed in on the other side, still neither saying a word. He somehow knew Rebecca would want it that way. When they finally reached the old farm house she finally spoke by telling him she could now walk on her own.

Dr. Brown got out of the car and walked around to the passenger's side. He opened the door and helped to get Rebecca out and onto her feet. He held on tight to her arm as he walked her up to her front door. He said,

"Rebecca, I will stay and tell the children."
He told her to please go lie down. Her legs were very weak, so she did just as he requested. She could hear as each one was told. Mabel screamed,

"NO, NO, NO!"
She could hear Dr. Brown say,

"I am so sorry baby, I wish I just could take away all of this pain from you and this family."
After listening for a few seconds, Rebecca knew her children needed her. She arose and staggered
230

into the parlor. She flopped into a chair. Mabel ran to her mother and hugged her. They both just cried. Her daughter then moved to the smaller children holding them as they were told one by one.

Dale Henderson came running into the parlor where his mother was dropped into a chair. He knew without being told what had happened. The look on everyone's face explained it all. He looked so very white as he ran to his mother and hugged her. The two of them both cried together for she does not know how long. She mustered up enough energy to tell him he must go up and tell his Aunt Ethel. As he took his hand from his mother's hands, they were both shaking. What more could this family bear?

It is a wonder the Dahl family got through still another funeral. In less than two years they had five wakes at their home. In less than two years they had attended five funerals. Rebecca had lost her husband, a sister-in-law and a brother-in-law. She had also lost two of her children. No one, including the family could figure out how they ever made it through the funerals. Now to deal with John Jr.'s as well. What a tragedy!

Thank God for that ever standing tree named Aunt Ethel. No one could ever love a sister-in-law more than Rebecca loved Ethel. The arrangements for this funeral were just given to Ethel. She planned everything. She worked with everyone while she too felt her heart breaking inside. She knew she had to stay strong. She knew Rebecca was now just a shell of a woman. Rebecca could hardly remember who was there, much less of how Ethel handled everything. She didn't even know what her other children were doing.    There was much concern for this devastated mother.  Everyone believed she went into a state of shock.  She could not remember anything.  All she knew was that she stayed numb. Even the youngest of children were just walking around in a daze.   No one talked to anyone. Nothing could be said that would ease any of this pain.  How could this be happening to one family? No one could tell them how sorry they were or that they understood, because they did not understand. Most people during the past two years seemed to want to avoid them as much as possible.  Maybe this was to be sure none of their bad luck would rub off onto them.  Now everyone was all there trying to comfort the family once more.  This time was so very different.  Not one person said much of anything, because you could tell no one knew what to say.

Rebecca could not even comfort her own children.  How could she help her neighbors and friends on what to say?  How could this family ever believe in anything ever again?  She thought she still believed in God, but as of right now she felt a big part of her own faith was shattered.  She needed to pray, but she did not have the strength. What would she pray about?  She had begged God to protect her family.  Now, it looked as if He was throwing them all away. The pastor came and prayed with her and thanked God for the years they were given with John, Jr.  She must have worded some of her feelings to the minister, because he kept telling her she must not lose her faith.  He kept saying things like,

"We do not understand these things, but God has a reason for everything."

232

Her thoughts were running wild as she tried to understand how one could understand a God who was taking her children. Her emotions were so destroyed she would weave between belief and hurt. Rebecca did remember saying,

"I love you Lord and remembered asking Him to please give her strength to go on."

Other than that, she does not remember praying much at all. All she could do was think of how could this happen and of how they could go on? What would they do now?

Once again all of the extended family members gathered at the Dahl home. Beatrice and her family came down. Mary, Eva, Dale and Chancy, along with all of their family members were at Rebecca's side. Everyone was there still once again to put part of her body, her heart and her very being into that old cold ground. The entire Dahl family was there as well. Both sides of these beautiful families had suffered so much from losing their loved ones in such a short span of time. Rebecca tried to be coherent because she knew her pain was not the only pain. None of the extended family members had said much of anything this time either. Everyone seemed to be locked into their very own kind of pain. Their reactions were pretty much the same as the immediate family. Everyone was sort of numb and seemed to be just going through the motions of the things that needed done. She watched each one of the family members break down into crumbs when they walked by the casket. She noticed different ones of them shaking someone's hand. She saw hugs and so on, but no one seemed to speak. They either held onto to each other very tightly or they just held their heads down in pain.

233

The undertaker's signs were once again put up in front of the house at each fork of the road. The signs once again stated that there was a death in the family. Once again wreaths were placed upon the doors. Once again the neighbors brought all kinds of food and everyone stayed up all night for a wake. It seemed this time everyone was so quiet. No one understood. No one could face the fact that another of this household had passed on. Everyone, including almost strangers just passed by the casket and said nothing. Each looked as if he or she were just in shock. Not one person said,

"I know how you feel."

Instead each person just looked at Rebecca. Many looked into her eyes as if they were scared to be around her and her destiny. Most showed in their eyes that they were feeling such deep pain for her. Silence was the only thing you could hear from anyone for the whole three days. It was obvious no one could believe that still another of the Dahl family had died in such a short time frame.

Ethel had pressed John, Jr.'s one and only suit. Everett had chosen a tie. James George and Dale Henderson just stood by the casket looking at their brother as if their feet were nailed to the floor. Someone did the chores. It must have been the neighbors. Rebecca thought for a brief moment that she must remember to thank them. Mary Bella and Edith stayed in one spot at the end of the couch during the days the body was at the home. They were not even moving their little feet or arms. This was so unusual for little children. Someone had dressed them in their best dresses and they looked like puppets or dolls that could not make a move. Rebecca realized she was not the only person in shock. The whole family most
234

surely was in shock. Everett's Hazel was there with a big part of her family. They were taking care of the food and trying to be sure everyone had something to eat. There was a never ending supply of handkerchiefs handed to Rebecca, but she did not know whether she was crying or not. She didn't believe she could cry anymore. She could just stare out into space.

That dreaded day came when the family was loading into the cars. The day of this funeral, no one had to tell anyone what car to get into. They were very well practiced. They seemed to follow some kind of a ritual as they funneled into each car. Rebecca had placed that green velvet dress upon her body once more and swore it was going to be burned when she got home. She refused to wear it to another funeral. At this point what was she to believe? Was the God that she had come to know and love going to take all of her children? What else was going to happen in her life?

Once the funeral started, Elizabeth once again, read some of Gwen's poems. Through her tears she told of how close her brother John and her sister Gwen were in life. She told of how she knew they would be so happy to see each other in Heaven. Everett spoke as well. He spoke of how he would miss his big brother. John Henderson tried to say something in behalf of his brother but could not say a word once he got up onto the podium. He just stood there for a minute saying nothing. Finally he said,

"You will have to excuse me and I'm sorry."

With that he walked down the one step and went straight to his mother. He was choked up but was able to talk with his mother. He said,

"Mother, I knew he was sick. If only I had told you! It is my fault he is dead."

Rebecca put her finger up to his lips as if to say, be still. She whispered,

"It is no one's fault. It is no one's fault!"

People filed one by one whilst stopping at the casket, then passing by this tragedy of a family. Many stopped to say,

"Rebecca, I am so sorry."

Many just hung their heads as they filed past the casket. At the end of the funeral service the family stood as long as they could keep their legs from shaking out from under them. They joined hands at the casket while they just stood their holding onto each other. Chancy walked up behind them and said the hearse was ready to go. Just like puppets on a string, each child and their mother filed out one by one. Elizabeth and her family marched out first, followed by Everett and Hazel, then the others. Once again they got into various cars that would carry them to where the other part of their household had been put to rest, that dreaded cemetery. Each family member could more than likely preach a funeral by now. Once again the sermon at the gravesite was,

"The Lord Givith. The Lord Takith away."

Rebecca did notice that the pastor did not even try to explain any reasoning as to why the Lord would want to take John, Jr. She knew he could not explain this one. She knew he had no reasoning any more than she did. He was very disturbed with the fact Rebecca was still losing one more. She could see many questions in his eyes. She

236

knew he wanted to ask God the very same question that she wanted to ask Him. She knew he would not ask that question any more than she would, in earnest anyway, because no one was to question their God.

# C hapter 20

The rest of the school year after February in 1934 was very tuff on everyone. The children were so torn up over still another death. Each child had to carry such a heavy work load at home and then go to school. James George's teacher had written home saying that she understood all of the family's problems and of how very sorry she was, but that James George was going to sleep in some of his classes. She stated that she needed Rebecca's help in solving this problem.

Everett had almost stopped visiting Hazel. Yet, when asked if everything was okay between them he would always answer with just a yes. He was beating himself up for not being there all the times he felt John, Jr. may have needed him. He was feeling John, Jr. had needed him so badly and that maybe he would have survived if he had given his brother more of his time. Thinking maybe less stress could have prevented the death. Rebecca told Everett this was not true, knowing her son could not live with those guilty feelings. She told him that John, Jr. would have asked him not to go when needed in the crops, or if he had needed him for help with the animals. She reminded him that John, Jr. had taken over the management of the farm rather well, and if he had needed him at those times he would have not been shy about demanding he be there. She did not want him to blame himself.

Rebecca knew Dale Henderson was trying really hard to blame himself as well. She knew deep in her heart, there was nothing anyone could have done. After reassuring Everett, she once again asked him about Hazel. He told his mother that he knew Hazel understood, but he had been feeling selfish by letting himself be with her. Rebecca told her son that Hazel was his future, his new life, and John, Jr. would not want him to lose any part of that happiness. She reminded him of how the whole family including John, Jr., father and Gwen had all loved Hazel and how she was sorry so much pain had to come into their relationship.

Things seemed to be getting back to normal as the school year continued. One day in March however, James George got off the school bus while Rebecca was watching out of the window. She noticed he did not wait for his sisters as he usually had done. Instead, he ran straight to the house. When James busted the kitchen door wide open, he was crying. He was a big boy for his age even though he was only twelve years old. It looked strange she supposed that a lad of his age would be so broken-up. Rebecca knew he would never let anyone see him cry, so she knew something was terribly wrong. She put her arms out for him and he fell right into them. He

240

wrapped his arms around his mother so tight she wasn't sure she could even breathe. She said,

"What on earth is wrong with you James?" He couldn't even speak for a while. He cried like his heart would surely break.

The other children came in the door with bewildered looks on their faces. Rebecca motioned for them to go on to the other part of the house. Finally she was able to get James to sit down upon a chair. She pulled another chair up facing him and took the bottom of her apron and wiped his eyes. He finally blurted out,

"Mother, the kids on the bus said they did not want to go by our house. They made funny sounds and said our house is The Death House." Rebecca's heart broke! She could tell something was terribly wrong but could have never guessed it was this. What could she say to comfort her son?

"Those children are just be being cruel," She said, but then almost said out loud.

"But they are so right! This is The Death House."

Rebecca concentrated on what she hoped would be the right thing to say to her young son. Finally she took his hands in hers and asked him to look into her eyes as she told him,

"I guess some people probably think this is a death house since we have lost so many of our family members."
She went on to say,

"It is very rare that a family would lose so many people in just two years, but you know what? Father, John, Jr., and Gwen are all up in Heaven looking down upon us right now. They don't want us to be sad. They are up there taking care of each other and they want us to take care of
241

each other down here. We will all go to Heaven to be with them someday. They will have made sure that they have a really nice place for all of us to live. I know it is hard to believe that right now, but we will see them again someday. Your little friends on the bus just don't understand. All they have seen is the signs along the roads and the wreaths upon our door."

After dinner Rebecca sat down in her husband's chair. She turned up the oil lamp and thought of James George being so disturbed that very day about what the children on the bus had said. She realized the unbearable pain she had gone through these past two years could only be magnified in a child's mind. She must try to protect the ones who are left. She must make them more comfortable and more understanding. That night, she called her children to her side and said,

"Tonight, instead of reading the Bible or another story; we are going to have a family chat. Everyone is going to be allowed to tell their fondest memory of their father, John, Jr. and Gwen."

Rebecca knew it was time for all to deal with their grief. Healing must begin. Hiding it inside of ones-self could only allow more out-bursts such as tonight. She started by saying that this would make them feel closer to their loved ones now that they are in Heaven. She was telling the children that the talking of their grief would help their loved ones rest as well.

"They too, will be happy when we remember the good times we had with them while they were alive. We need to do this instead of covering ourselves in so much grief to where we don't even know how to live."

242

She stated that she knew this was exactly what father, John and Gwen would want. She then said,

"I have it on good authority and have a hunch that they are watching our little pow'wow right now. So gather around."

As each child found a place on a couch, chair or the floor, Rebecca said,

"Who wants to go first?"

No one moved to say anything. James looked like he wanted to talk least of all, but with a little probing he started talking. Before long he sounded so grown up. It was as if he were preaching a sermon or doing a book report at school. The dry eyed little man did not have to stand on a stool anymore. He was taller than his brother Dale Henderson. He was a big strong, muscle looking child. He stood up to talk with his shoulders back and standing proud. Rebecca was so proud of him. She had not meant for this gathering to be so formal, but James started off by saying,

"I was the seventh child born to John and Rebecca Dahl."

Everyone laughed at the way he started his speech. Someone made the remark that,

"Hey they knew that he was born the seventh child."

This did not seem to trouble him. He went on with his story. He said,

"Eventually, my parents had nine children."

He proceeded in naming each and everyone in the order they were born. Some of the older children were raising an eyebrow and some smiles could be seen, but Rebecca felt much pride as her youngest son had the complete attention of his brothers and sisters. Even Everett and Mabel showed him the

243

respect he so deserved for this performance. Rebecca assumed he was talking in this way because he had pretended to be a preacher for so long. He was more comfortable with this way of explaining himself. Just as if he had a script before him, James George stated of how he was raised on a farm in Southern Ohio and of how his family dug their living and their food out of the ground. Rebecca almost smiled because he had decided to go way back. It did not seem to matter. None of the other children seemed to care if they talked or not. By now, they were captivated by their little brother's speech. He continued by telling of how before the coming of buses, they had walked many miles to a small county school each day. They returned home to find mother cooking a big pot of beans or potatoes. He told of how they worked very hard and of how they never went hungry. As this now young man went on with his auto-biography; each child started to act as though they were letting some of their grief out of their systems. They seemed to be comforted just by listening to their now, seeming wise little brother.

"God is good to us,"
James proclaimed. He looked at his mother and said,

"Training about Jesus has soaked into me, and I am so thankful to be raised in a Christian home."
He said,

"I am thankful the Lord saw fit to let me know my father and to know Gwen and John, Jr."
He looked around to the others and said,

"He did not have to let us have them at all you know, but He did."
244

Everyone was crying now, including James George. But through his tears he was also smiling at his remembrance of his loved ones. Rebecca noticed she had a smile upon her face as well. She thought of how James George would truly do great things in his life, because she too was feeling comforted by a mere child's speech. She looked around and saw each of her children smiling too. It was as if a ray of sunshine came through to all of them on that night. Rebecca knew it was the presence of God.

It was as if James George was touched by God. It felt like he had a view into Heaven. When he sit down the others wanted to speak. As each child spoke of the wonderful times they had spent with each missing member of their family. It became a very nice night. They started telling funny things they had done to each other and funny things the others had done to them. Rebecca was surprised to hear some of the jokes they had all pulled on each other. They laughed about how Daddy always said if you don't work you don't eat and of how he would threaten to spank one of them many times only to give them that dreaded lecture instead. Everyone agreed of how they would have rather taken the spanking. Dale Henderson told of when he got into trouble he would always try to make it right by pruning something. Mary Bella spoke up and said,

"Mommy, I call him Johnny Apple-Seed." They all laughed.

James George must have thought this was a time to tell of all their sins as well. He stood up again with the same determination as his first speech. He spoke of how sorry he was for different little things he had done. He reminded
245

the family of their winter trips to the church. He told of how he had often played opossum when the car would not make it up the hills. He mentioned how father would make the other children get out and walk up the hill so the car would make it. He would often pretend to be asleep, thus guaranteeing he would not have to get out in the cold. He also told his siblings for the first time of what was said on the bus about their house being the death house. It surprised Rebecca he would share this with the other children as she thought he would be embarrassed that he had cried over it. Rebecca could see the sadness and hurt come over each child's face. Then, Edith Bea spoke up and said, "But I will bet none of them have a handsome brother like mine."

Rebecca did not know what that had to do with anything, but was very thankful for the outburst because it caused the room to fill with laughter. Laughter was what was needed so badly in this family now. That night was a healing night. Rebecca knew this as she listened to each child's remembrance of their loved ones. As Everett was finishing up his talk, he looked around and thanked each child for getting along so well with each other. James said he was sorry for being the more ornery of all. Rebecca spoke up and reassured him that there was not enough time for anyone to get into too much meanness as each child had so many chores to do.

Rebecca started analyzing the evening once everyone else was in bed. The hardest part of all their stories was when they were telling of what age they each were when their father died. Mabel had stated,

"Fortunately, our mother is a great manager."

She was repeating words she had heard her brother John say on many occasions. Rebecca marveled in the realization that her children sounded so grown up, but was sad for that very same reason. She had allowed the conversions to continue way past bed time. They needed to get all of their feelings out into the open.

Rebecca had taught a very strong will to each of her children. She had instilled in them that anything anyone of them had to say was very important. She truly believed each of them to be well rounded individuals. This night no one tried to stop the tears. They cried, they laughed and they prayed in a circle to God and thanked Him for caring for those gone on. They asked him to protect the rest of their family. As each child stood up so bravely to tell their story; they were releasing so much pain and yet while holding onto their precious memories. They were healing each other. Though she never thought possible, Rebecca could feel the healing process begin within her. She could feel her faith coming back. The pride and the blessings she felt from listening to these beautiful children swept slowly over her whole body. She knew in her heart she was still very blessed, still truly blessed indeed.

# C hapter 21

At the end of the school year, Rebecca had to pull Dale Henderson and James George out early. She knew Dale Henderson would not be going back to school the following year. This broke her heart, but she had no other choice. Probably within another year she would have to pull James George out as well. Maybe someday they could complete their education. Right now they were farmers and they had to become men. Rebecca often felt so very badly about her children having to grow up so fast. They never had much of a chance to be children.

Mabel did get to go to Huntington, West Virginia to work and train for nursing. John, Jr. had insisted she do just that. Rebecca chose to honor his wishes even though she could have used her at home. Her young male friend was not too happy with anyone over that decision, but was always very happy when she came home to visit. Rebecca realized there would be a wedding there before long.

Elizabeth came over every chance she got. She would teach the children little songs she taught in school. This was good for the children because their house did not need to be such a sad house. Mary Bella would walk around the house singing about a little ducky duttle and Edith Bea would sing something about whether her ears were on straight or not. Rebecca appreciated her daughter Elizabeth so much for trying to keep some cheer in the little ones hearts.

On the first day of September they attended the very beautiful wedding of Everett Dahl and Hazel Nash. They had a reception on the grounds of the Danville Church. Everyone was so happy for the new married couple. The Dahl children were all very happy that the couple would be living just down the road on the very same farm. Rebecca felt sorry for Hazel's family because they would not see her as often. What was that old saying?

"You gain a son but lose a daughter." Regardless, Rebecca was very pleased to have Hazel as her new daughter-in-law. Time passed in a healthy, happy sort of way. In 1935, Everett and Hazel had their first child and named him John. Rebecca was so happy about that. She was enjoying having grandchildren of her very own. The family was growing again.

Then in 1936 Elizabeth had another child. This was the very first granddaughter. Rebecca still had five children at home, but tried to devote as much time as possible to her grandchildren. The Dahl children were so self-sufficient anymore. She sometimes felt they could carry on without her.

Mabel was home again. Bryon Wyman had broken an arm. Rebecca knew this young couple was truly in love when her daughter refused to return to St. Mary's for a while after a week-end

250

visit. She was determined to stay home and take care of her beau. Rebecca was okay with this decision as Mabel was a wonderful helper around the house and in the fields.

Everett had taken over the role of manager of the farm. Dale Henderson and James George followed every direction their big brother Everett gave them. He really took charge after John, Jr.'s death. With great management and hard work; they kept that old farm going at full speed.

During the 1930's, the 'Great Depression' hit the country with a bang. Everyone was so devastated. But at the Dahl farm they kept raising their own food and other than having a hard time getting sugar or something like that, their life went on as usual.

After several months of the daughter Mabel returning home, Rebecca found that she and Bryon Wyman had secretly married. When asked why they ran off to do such a thing, Rebecca was told it was so she would not have to worry with a wedding. She knew in her heart the young lady was almost afraid to show happiness around the Dahl farm. She also knew she must do something to change that.

During the next years, crops were planted and crops were reaped. James George did have to quit school. This broke Rebecca's heart, but she had to have the help on the farm. Everyone seemed very well adjusted. Each child was growing up too fast. Mabel and Bryon Wyman had moved into an old share cropper's house that was on the border of the Wyman and Dahl farms. This was something that worried Rebecca and Mrs. Wyman because this house was way back off the road and Mabel would walk through the fields

251

each day to come help her mother. Their worries were doubled when they were told by Mabel and Bryon that there was going to be a new grandchild before long.

Edith was in High School now and would graduate shortly thereafter and Bella was right behind her in the growing up department. James George was nineteen already. He had been spending a lot of his spare time at his sister Elizabeth's. He adored Simon and went to play with him often. He seemed to be the entire group of grandchildren's favorite uncle. Rebecca believed it was because he could get down on their level and be just as silly as they, when called upon to do so.

Rebecca did not know whether the visits to Elizabeth's had caused it, or the visits to Elizabeth's were because of it. But, about 1940 or 1941 James George brought home a very pretty little blonde from that area. She was only sixteen or seventeen but seemed much more mature. Rebecca found she was the daughter of a new minister at the church where Elizabeth and her family attended. Before long James George would take the Model T and go to Danville every chance he got. Everett would often complain about his disappearances. Rebecca would laugh and remind him that history sometimes repeats itself. She told him of how she could not see a difference in James George's reactions over the recent devotions of him to Hazel. She reminded him of some other trips that old Model T had made to Danville. Laughing about the strange draw that little town had on her sons.

February 06, 1943, James and his little blonde were married. The minister who was

Lucille's father performed the ceremony in their living room, then they had a reception under a large pretty tree. Rebecca knew her son would be very happy. She was happy for him and this is one wedding where she did not even cry. Maybe part of the reason was because James was not moving away. Lucille would be moving in with them. Rebecca had tried to decorate the upstairs in a way for privacy and hopefully comfort for the new bride. It would probably be hard on the young lady since she hardly knew any of the family. Edith and Bella shared the big bedroom downstairs by now. Dale Henderson had taken the small bedroom and Rebecca slept in the parlor most of the time.

Within the following year, Dale Henderson had met a young lady from West Virginia and married her. He then moved to Columbus, Ohio to finish his education and pursue a career of his choice. His wife was also a beauty. Rebecca could not help but think of how handsome her sons must be. They sure had attracted beautiful women. All three of her daughter-in-laws were extremely beautiful young ladies. By now she had lots of beautiful grandchildren as well.

Edith graduated from High School. She then also moved to Columbus, Ohio. She lived with her brother and his wife as she started her career in life. Bella was still at home and in her last year of school when James George had his first child. It was a girl. Bella became so attached to this new baby. She would tell everyone that was the prettiest baby she had ever seen. Rebecca remembered her thoughts from years ago believing each of her children upon their birth, was the prettiest child ever born. She had to laugh as she thought of how history really does repeat itself.

After Bella graduated, she too moved to Columbus, Ohio. She and her sister rented an apartment together just as Rebecca and Beatrice, Alice and Gwen had done years before. Rebecca knew they must have had great fun together. After a year or so, both of the girls had met and married the men of their dreams.

James George would never leave the farm. He stayed with his mother and managed the farm for many years. Three of his four children were born on that farm. The two oldest were born in the very same small bedroom as he. The third child was born in a hospital. People were doing more of that by this time.

As years went by, farming was not enough to keep a family going during the modern times. James had to start looking for other ways of making money for his mother and his family. He chose to sell kitchen gas stoves from a catalog. He went all over the county side selling stoves. He would then come home at nights to do all of his chores around the farm. He was an ambitious young man, so within a few years he had managed to save enough money to buy a property in the small town named after his ancestors. This town was only two miles away from the farm, but to watch Rebecca's reactions one would have believed it was as far away as Columbus.

When James and Lucille's oldest child was in the third grade they moved into their new home. James had built this home with his own two hands. He was a large strong man. He was bigger than any of Rebecca's other children. He was a very handsome dark headed man. Rebecca was so very proud of him.

Rebecca never gained any weight and the stress and hard work over the years had taken its toll on her. She was becoming sickly a lot anymore. Many times she was unable to go to church. One time just before the move to the new house all of the children were called in from their homes because Rebecca almost died. She had something wrong with her lungs. Water would build up around her heart. The family rushed in! They prayed over her all night. She was so near death to where all the children knew only God had spared her. After that, she would sometimes have to stay in bed for days. She was not being realistic with her thoughts of staying on the farm by herself, but the move was killing her. She became so very depressed.

On the last day of the move, Rebecca took her good ole time getting out of the house. James had told her that she could come over with him twice a day to do the chores if she wished. He explained to his mother that nothing was leaving the house but their clothes. He assured her they were not giving up farming. He would continue to run the farm. He felt very sad that night as he watched his mother's face when he told her they now had to go. She had dressed warm as she always did. She had a pretty silk scarf tied tightly around her chin. The sun was setting, leaving a beautiful glow over the old home place. As James threw the last suit-case into the back of the truck, he turned to see his mother's back. She was standing there looking back at her house. She had his oldest two children on each side of her while holding their little hands in hers. He knew she was crying. Her thoughts were racing over all the years she had spent living at this old farm. She felt as if that farm was as important to her as breathing. She had loved so much and lost so much upon this old farm. Her heart was now breaking.

Shortly after their move, Rebecca was once more the proud new owner of her mother's organ. Her younger sister had moved and no longer had room for the beautiful old piece of furniture. Lucille made room for this large item in her small new modern living room. Lucille could not have been happier to have been in her new home. She had lived with her mother-in-law for ten years and was so very happy to finally have a home of her own. She knew Rebecca's heart was breaking, but she still could not hide her excitement over her new home.

Rebecca had stopped that very idea once before. James and Lucille had built a tiny little home on the lower part of the farm before their first child was born. It was close to Everett and Hazel. Rebecca had all but refused for them to move into it. She became very sick and the couple left their little house empty for the rest of the days. Now the time had come to have a nice new home and they were moving in and taking Rebecca along with them. The least Lucille could do was make room for that antique organ. Her choices were of a modern furniture in bright blonde colors, but when she took the large top off the organ and placed pictures across the top, it fit in pretty well.

After a while Rebecca settled into her fate. There were many days she would just enjoy her grandchildren. She would play the old organ and sing old songs with the children. For the first time

256

in her adult life, she did not have to work her fingers to the bone and she should have been happy to be comfortable. James and Lucille even had indoor plumbing and all of the new modern ideas. For most people this would have been nice. To Rebecca she just felt lost, so very lost. After the first few years her illness and probably her depression caused her to just go to bed. The doctors came and went while telling the family she had just lost her will to live. As time passed, she became very weak. After a year or so Rebecca was not even able to get out of bed. The doctors gave her condition a term called 'bedfast'.

The big loving family visited with their mother almost every weekend. By this time Everett and Hazel had also moved away. They had purchased a dairy farm not many miles out of Columbus. Rebecca's children were all successful and all seemed to be very happy. Though she felt her life was over, one could tell she was very proud of her children. The grandchildren were growing up fast. All were healthy and beautiful. She could not help but notice the grandchildren acted the same as her children. She was overwhelmed with the thoughts of how wonderful all of them got along so well. The families visited so much to where the cousins were all more like brothers and sisters, more so than like cousins. She would often laugh to herself as she would hear one or another of her children getting onto the grandchildren for something they were doing. She thought it was funny of how none of them seemed to just correct their own child or even act as though any one of them was theirs more than the other. It was as if each child had many parents and all were corrected the same and by everyone.

257

As for the home place, no one ever dared to remove one item from Rebecca's house. Somewhere along the line someone got the bright idea that they believed would make their mother happier. So, each summer the children would take turns with their vacations and stay at the old farm house. This gave Rebecca each whole summer there. They would prop her up in the window of that old parlor. She was surrounded by all of her own belongings and one could tell this made her very happy. Then when winters came, she must go to one of the children's. She stayed with James George for a couple of years. Then the other children felt they should take turns. She went to live with Mabel for a while. She lived with Edith a while then onto Everett and Hazel's.

This huge family loved, laughed and planned their lives right beside of their mother's bedside for several years. No one would have ever dreamed of not including this strong loving woman in every phase of their lives. During her lifetime, Rebecca was lucky to never lose another child. She went on to have twenty-two grandchildren. She had to laugh at herself when old habits never changed. With each new birth she would tell everyone that she knew for sure this was the prettiest child the family had delivered to date. There was only one child she did not get to see, but she knew he was coming. She loved each and every one of her grandchildren with all of her heart.

The years before Rebecca moved in with James George, and the summers staying at the farm gave each grandchild the memories that her own children had so enjoyed. The old farm had become magical. John, Sr., John, Jr., Gwen and the others were surly watching over this wonderful old piece of dirt. Rebecca loved watching her grandchildren doing the very same things her children had done years before. She noticed her children did not cut them any slack even though they did not have to work quite as hard as her children had to do. She did notice each of her children repeating all the same things she and John had instilled upon them. She would chuckle when she would hear one of her children scream out,

"You don't work, we don't eat."

She could not help but notice how no one sorted out the children. She sometimes felt sorry for her grandchildren because it often looked to her as if they had a whole yard full of bosses. She would then laugh at herself for going soft and realize these children knew no better and they seemed to love every minute of it.

Rebecca ended up with the most wonderful, loved and respected family in the county, and she became a legend in her own time. As noted, she never married again, nor even had another gentleman in her life. She lived for her children, her grandchildren and her God. She tried to raise each of them to prepare for Heaven. She believed with all of her heart that is where they would all be together once more. This beautiful lady was somehow able to connect the two, Heaven and earth. As author of this book and one of the grandchildren of one such lovely lady, while telling this story I often realize as a child I was not able to distinguish between the two. One was the earth you could see and Heaven was where the other part of the family lived and we would all go visit them someday. It was as if Rebecca always lived somewhere in between. She became a pillar of her community and a backbone of her church. This lady lived through many, many sorrows, a world depression and two world wars. Many would have collapsed or given up, but she stayed strong just as long as she could. It looked as if she had given up a little after she no longer felt useful, but this was so far from the truth. She pushed on to teach her beliefs and bestowed her love upon everyone who was fortunate enough to come in contact with her.

Dahl children still play on that beautiful old farm. Every generation will forever have the memories of the beautiful place Rebecca made home. October the 6th of 1958 Rebecca Dahl went home to be with John, John, Jr., Gwen, her other loved ones and her God. The family dressed this lovely lady in a beautiful full length flowing lavender gown and placed an orchid upon her. She had told everyone not to feel sad about her leaving because she was just going home. We sent her to meet John Dahl looking just as beautiful as she had that day he met her at that old train station so many years ago. This time, we are sure John had removed any trees that may have adorned her Heavenly living room long before she ever arrived.

Those left behind will forever be saddened by the realization that we will never again hear those high heels ping across that concrete patio, nor will we hear Rebecca shout,

"Get Up, You're Burning Sunshine!"

Those of us left behind wonder what the world would have been like without this beautiful daughter, mother and grandmother. We wonder how we could have faced all the trials this woman had to face. She was born in the lap of luxury, only to become a dirt farmers wife. Never once did that fact trouble this lovely lady. She made her world so rich with love.

Rebecca was a faithful loving devoted daughter, mother, grandmother, mother-in-law and wife. Her son James completed his education and <u>DID</u> go on to become a country minister, just as she had predicted. Although this did not happen until awhile after she had passed. We all know she probably had some way of knowing this. As the years passed, several of her grandsons and grandson-in-laws became ministers as well. We know she is very proud of all of her children and her grandchildren. The belief system she instilled, the faith, the honesty and high moral standards she held so dear have been followed as she wished throughout her beautiful family. Each and every one of her children lived their lives in the most wholesome, wonderful way. Just as she had so desired. The strong impression this tiny little lady left upon her children and the world around her will never be forgotten.

At Dale Henderson's funeral one cousin asked another;

"How do we explain our family to other people? Our grandmother, uncles and aunts were the closest family one could ever know. And how do you explain, or why would anyone ever believe that they lived their lives the nearest to perfect that any mortal persons on earth could."

No one can remember one harsh word or a wrong doing. The weight of the world was upon this woman's petite little shoulders, but she weathered all of the storms and raised a family to be so proud of. Everyone who ever knew her, or any of her children will always remember each and every one of them with complete love and admiration. Rebecca Dahl shined and 'thank God', she never once *Burned her Sunshine*!

Rebecca Dahl 1883-1958

*TRAGEDIES OF THE DAHL'S*
consists of a group of three books:
**BURNING SUNSHINE, HONORABLE LIFE**
**&**
**THE REVEREND'S DAUGHTER**
The three books are based on a true Southern Ohio family.

Considered Fiction – However - Actual people did live these lives. The names have been changed. There are three generations of this family written about in the three books. The women who were the inspiration for Mary Bella and James George's wife (Lucy) are alive and in their mid-eighties. Many of the third, fourth and fifth generation family members live in Ohio. Several still live on that wonderful old farm in Gallia County. The author who lives in Ohio and Georgia is a member of that family.

The author writes only Historical Fiction Novels and fun children's books since the *Tragedies of the Dahl's* were complete. The love, the tragedies, faith and hope of this family was such a unique story, the author felt this story had to be told first. The hope was that these books would inspire others to be more thankful, more caring and more devoted to their faith and happiness. Based on the comments and reviews, it looks like the author has accomplished her wish. This amazing family is what caused this retired accountant to become an author.

Receiving great reviews & comments!
The author truly appreciates your comments about her book. Messages can be left on the web-site or storefront.

www.ingramcontent.com/pod-product-compliance
Lightning Source LLC
Chambersburg PA
CBHW031106260626
47172CB00001B/242